Max Justice:
Vengeance

Bob Goodwin

© 2019

Bob Goodwin

ISBN: 978-0-6481533-2-0 (paperback)

ISBN: 978-0-6481533-3-7 (eBook)

Bob Goodwin AUSTRALIA

Cover design by

Spiffing Covers

enquiries@spiffingcovers.com

For Jenny

CHAPTER 1

MR *JONES*

A silver Mercedes A-Class hatch parked on the side of a suburban street underneath a broken street light. Inside, a middle-aged man in a suit and tie waited. On the passenger's seat, next to a roll of masking tape, lay several black leather ligatures, each about fifty centimetres long.

It was eight-forty in the evening, thirty minutes after sunset, and a pleasant fifteen degrees, when a lime green Toyota Starlet entered the quiet street in Lambton, Newcastle.

Angelique Hawke, a personal trainer at the local gym, parked on the cement tracks of number twenty-eight, then made her way with her gym bag to the front door of her low-set home. She opened the unlocked screen door, pushed her key into the deadlock and turned the door handle.

The suited man hardly made a sound as he grabbed her around the waist with one arm and around her mouth with his other. He marched her through the opening door, then pushed it closed with his foot.

She tried to bite his hand, then tried to twist and kick back with her feet. She attempted to grab at him with her arms as she squealed. He swept her legs from under her and threw her, face first, to the floor. He straddled her back and pushed her face hard against the threadbare rug.

'If you behave you won't be harmed,' he said loudly with his face near hers. 'I will tie your hands and feet and cover your eyes. That is all I will be doing. But if you are disagreeable you will feel pain and lose blood. Do we have an understanding?'

Angelique nodded as best she could. 'Yes. Don't hurt me. Please. I am a good person. I don't have much money, but you can have it,' she whimpered. 'Are you going to rape me?'

'I don't want any money or possessions. And I have no plans to sexually assault you, but I do want your hands behind your back.' The man had a clear, calm and authoritative voice which gave her no reassurance. Angel moved her hands behind her.

'Okay, there you are.' She put her hands onto her lower back. 'I'm cooperating. You don't need to hurt me.' He secured her wrists with the leather ties. She lay still while he bound her ankles and then placed tape over her eyes. He rolled her over, stood her up, and supported her to take a few short shuffling steps backwards, then sat her on the lounge.

The tall man stood there staring at her as she shook, over-breathed and turned her head side to side trying to work out where he was. Her suited attacker was a handsome man in his forties with neat short cut black hair and shiny black leather shoes.

'Who are you?' said Angel with a high-pitched trembling voice. 'What do you want from me?'

'You can call me Jones,' replied the man as he checked out his surroundings.

The interior of the suburban home was tidy but dated, worn and in need of a refurb. An "L" shaped laminated kitchen bench served as a partition between kitchen and lounge and doubled as a breakfast bar/dining area. He dragged a bar stool away from the bench.

'I want to talk to you about Robert Mallory,' he finally said as he hopped up on the stool and sat in front of, and above her.

'Robbie! Really? He's been gone for months. The bastard owes me a shitload of rent. I've spoken to the cops already. I have no idea where he is.'

'Yes, I know all that.'

'I'm really scared,' whimpered Angel. 'I still think you are going to hurt me.'

'Really? I just reassured you. Why would you still think that?'

'Because I am tied up and you don't want me to see your face. Which is good. I don't want to see it, really I don't,' she said rapidly. 'And I don't know what you're doing or about to do.' Angel turned her head trying to tune in to any sound.

'You just try to relax and talk to me then we will get along just fine.'

'I am pretty sure I don't have the answers you want. Robbie was not very friendly. Never said a lot. Went to work came home, kept to himself. Went out overnight from time to time. Never said where he was going…' Angel hesitated. 'Huh…'

'Huh, what?'

'You and him… please don't be offended Mister Jones, but… partners maybe? He was a bit different. Always thought he was gay.'

'No. Colleagues to a degree I guess, but not partners in the sense that you're suggesting. And nothing you say will offend me.'

'Colleagues at what?'

'Tell me about when he disappeared,' he said completely ignoring her question.

'There's nothing to tell. I came home from work and he wasn't here. He had been here because his work backpack was here. That's all there is to it.'

'Did anything unusual happen on that day or around that time? Did he have any visitors or phone calls that you remember?'

'No…well maybe Carl, that's his brother who lives three doors up. That would be all. Why don't you go and see him? He's an arse too, just like Robbie.'

'I have spoken to Carl. A very rude man. And he wasn't very forthcoming. Did *you* have any visitors around this time? Any strangers come to the door? Anything that may have been a bit out of the ordinary?'

Angel took a moment then tipped her head to one side. 'Actually, yes. A couple of days after he disappeared a very attractive man came to see me.'

'Okay,' said the suited man as he took out his mobile phone and opened a voice record app.

'He was really nice, tall, tanned. Long blonde hair and a goatee. Strong. Had his arm in a sling. Ray that was his name. Yeah, he stood me up…twice! The world is full of arseholes.'

'Very poor form. Now this might be important. I want to know everything about this "Ray" guy. What he said. What you did together. Other features of his body or face. If you had ever seen him before or since.'

'Will you let me go then? After I tell you.'

'If you tell me everything and don't lie, yes I'll let you go. Promise.'

Angel started describing her first meeting with Ray, which was before Robbie disappeared, when he arrived at the gym looking for a personal trainer and displaying a photo of Mallory.

'He was so gorgeous looking,' said Angel. 'It seems odd now I talk about it, but at the time it seemed innocent enough. He rang me that evening with a plan to meet for a drink, but he disappeared only to turn up at my door two days later with his arm in a cast and a story about being hit by a motorcycle.'

'Did he have a surname?'

'I never knew his full name.'

'Did you fuck him?'

'Oh shit. Please don't think bad of me, but I really wanted to. I thought he wanted me too, but he pissed off while I was in the shower waiting for him.'

'Did he take or steal anything? Did he ask you any questions?'

'Really, he didn't seem overly inquisitive. Don't think he pinched anything. Nothing of mine. I have no idea what shit Mallory had in his room. It's possible.'

'Where is that shit now?'

'Boxed up in the corner of my room. Go knock yourself out.'

It had been months since *Jones* had heard from Mallory, and while he cared little for the guy, his absence could be an indicator of possible problems.

He paused his phone recording, left Angel on the couch, moved to her bedroom and worked his way through the boxes, upending the contents over her bed. There were clothes, clean and dirty, three pairs of shoes, some magazines on fitness and a couple of porn mags, DVDs, a few documents and receipts that he checked and discarded. There was the backpack and a small suitcase containing towels, sheets, toiletries and a few more clothes. There was a wallet with fifty dollars, driver's licence and credit cards. There was a laptop cable and mouse but no laptop computer.

Jones grunted and returned to the lounge where Angel sat quietly. The pace of her breathing had settled somewhat. He continued the recording of his interview.

'There is no phone there,' he said.

'The police took that. Said they would do some checks on it.'

'There is no laptop either.'

'He definitely had one. The cops could've taken that too. I don't know. I only noticed them leave with the phone. There was not one in his room when I packed up his crap.'

Jones pulled a flick knife from his pocket and threw it open. The blade clicked into place. 'Is there anything more you can tell me about Ray, Mallory or anything else? Take your time.'

'I just heard a metal sound. What was that? Was it a blade? I've been honest with you. Please Mr Jones!'

'Anything else at all, Miss Hawke?'

'Are you going to kill me? Please… I don't want to die, Mister

Jones.'

'I need you to be focused. Sometimes fear helps. The sound was a flick knife. I am holding it in my hand. I don't want to harm you. I am not normally a violent man.' Jones lifted the blade and turned it in his hands. It had smears of blood on both sides. He stood and stepped towards his captive. He placed the side of the cold metal against her cheek. She gasped and pulled away. 'Think. Please, Angel.'

She panted and screwed up her face. Some tears found their way under the tape and ran down the sides of her nose. 'He rang me,' she panted. 'When I was nearly at my front door. Ray called me and invited me for a drink at Bar 121. I had given him my number – wrote it on a brochure and gave it to him when I first met him at the gym.'

'Was Mallory home?'

'Probably, the lights were on inside. He would often be here when I got home.'

'You didn't enter the house?'

'No. I went straight back to my car and off to Bar 121.'

'You normally give guys your number and take off like that when they call you?'

'I am known to be a bit forward. But this guy… Ray. He was a real honey… and… as I told you…'

'Yes, you wanted to fuck him. Do you still have his phone number?'

'I do. But it's disconnected. I've called it a dozen times.'

'I'll be wanting the number anyway.'

'It's in my phone.'

Jones pulled Angel forward. She squealed. 'And where is your phone, sweetheart?'

'My gym bag. In the side pocket. Please,' she gasped. 'I am doing everything you ask. I am being truthful.'

Jones found her phone. She squealed again when he grabbed her right hand and pushed her thumb against the bottom button. The screen opened. He opened her contacts and scrolled through to the letter R.

'It's not under "R", Angel!'

'Under G. Look under G for Gorgeous. Ray Gorgeous.'

Jones found the name and read out the number, so it was recorded. He cut the ties around her wrists. 'Stay seated. Leave the tape on for five minutes. Clear?'

'Yes, yes. Thank you. Yes.'

'It is likely the police may drop around again to have a chat with you. It would be in your best interests to keep my visit to yourself. Then I would have no reason to return.'

'I know nothing. I will not be talking to anyone. Promise.' She took a deep breath. 'I'd like to ask a question if I could.'

'Ask away,' said Jones with a shrug of his shoulders.

'Do you think Mallory left with Ray? Sorry, just wondering. You know, for my own peace of mind. And I want to know if I'll ever see the money he owes me.'

There was a moment of silence. Jones gazed at her. He flicked the knife closed. Angel finally let herself fall back on the lounge.

'I am close to certain that this *Ray* person abducted Mallory then came back for the laptop. There is no chance of you getting any cash back. And I'm not sure how much peace of mind it will give you, but I believe Mallory has been murdered.'

'Ray a murderer! Why, Mr Jones?'

'No more questions. Goodbye Angel. The tape stays on for five minutes, right.'

'Five minutes. Yes. I got it,' she nodded.

Jones grunted and left.

CHAPTER 2

FAMILY AFFAIRS

Kourtney and Khloe Kearsley's mother, Karen, was a huge fan of the Kardashian family and had ignored conventional spelling protocols by so naming her twin girls, and her younger son Kris, to match the socialites and wait in hope of similar fame and fortune. In 2009, she legally changed Courtney and Chloe's names by deed poll. Unfortunately, the attention she desired for herself and her girls, and the attention they ultimately received, were not quite what Karen had in mind.

Kourtney and Khloe were slender nineteen-year-olds with their original long mousy brown locks now bleached blonde. Today they had dressed in casual clothes; faded jeans with stylish rips and holes, white t-shirts and Nikes. They also wore something neither had ever worn before – a full length plastic apron.

The sisters squeezed each other in a tight embrace and quietly cried on each other's shoulder. They both had bandages on their wrists.

'We can do this,' said Kourtney.

'We can do this,' echoed Khloe, beginning her reply just before her sister had finished speaking.

'We must do it,' said Kourtney.

'We must,' replied Khloe.

The twins stood in a large, well lit room with concrete walls and a polished concrete floor. Along one wall were shelves and pegboards with every imaginable electrical and carpentry tool, all neatly displayed and ready for use.

This was the underground bunker of Maxwell Judd. A place where victims could meet their offenders on their own terms and serve out a form of justice more appropriate than a brief prison sentence, court directed community service, a fine or getting off scot-free on a technicality.

Four weeks ago, and at the insistence of their mother, the twins had responded to an internet add offering good money and future opportunities in the modelling and television industries for the right person. They both presented for interviews at what appeared to be a legitimate office in Ryde, Sydney. There were several male and female staff at the agency and the girls were put through their paces in front of a panel of interviewers then photographed in different clothing against various backdrops. They both handed over six-hundred dollars for photo shoot costs and proofs then left with some expectation of hearing back within a week or two.

And indeed, a week later, they both heard back on the same day. Kourtney in the morning then Khloe in the early afternoon. The photographer, Salvatore Lombardi, told each of the girls they had made the final top ten and invited them to a private address for a final series of photos to help the firm make its decision.

By mid-afternoon Lombardi had both girls chained in a basement. He whipped, cut and beat them before forcing them to perform sexual acts on each other – then he raped them and left them for dead, chained up in a house where the owners were away on a three-month overseas holiday. It was the girls' mother, Karen, who contacted police that evening when they had not returned home and were not answering their phones. When finally rescued, the twins were damaged – probably more so emotionally than physically. They spent a night in hospital together before being discharged with arrangements in place for counselling and community support visitations.

Two days later the girls believed their lives were over. They had let their mother down, they were dirty, damaged, unlovable and unemployable. They made a suicide pact.

The twins planned their deaths for when their mother was out buying clothes. They positioned two poolside sun chairs next to each other in a vacant garage space, then they each took ten Valium tablets. They knew the dose would not kill them, but it would take the edge off their anxiety and allow them to doze off and drift away into reincarnation. When the girls began to feel drowsy, they closed all the garage doors and turned on the engine of the one remaining car. Next, they both placed a bucket next to their sun lounges, cut their wrists and hung their bleeding arm into the bucket. They clasped their free hands together, looked into each other's eyes and cried as they faded away.

It was a near perfect plan, but three things went wrong. Firstly, they had not switched off the air-conditioning, so the amount of carbon monoxide never reached a lethal level. Secondly, after an hour the car ran out of fuel and stopped. And, thirdly, the cuts to their wrists, after bleeding profusely at first, slowed down and clotted due to the coolness of the air and their slow pulse rate from the Valium.

They were taken by ambulance and admitted to the psychiatric ward where they spent three days.

Police investigating the case discovered that the agency had sacked Lombardi a few days earlier and that "Lombardi" was not even his real name.

He had managed to elude the police. Max Judd, however had a somewhat persuasive, and ultimately successful, after-hours chat with an agency colleague of Lombardi's and managed to get the guy's new mobile number. The rest was child's play – sending him a text about another attractive *wanna be* film star and setting up a meeting.

Now, Lombardi, AKA John Watson, and not even of Italian heritage, was secured on Max's table; held down by tension straps; his head in a vice and a black rubber ball gag wedged in his mouth. His eyes and nose were covered by a heavy piece of leather about the size of a placemat.

Kourtney switched on the hand-held paint burner and moved towards him. Khloe had put on some heavy-duty gloves to carry the bottle of sulphuric acid. She placed it on the table next to Lombardi's head. The paint burner was a hand-held tool a little like a cordless drill but with an open silver nozzle at one end. There was no visible flame. The device expelled super-heated air capable of burning paint from surfaces, melting plastics and charring raw timber.

Kourtney threw the cover from the man's eyes. On seeing his face, she took a step back and gasped. It was more in shock than fear on seeing the man that had damaged her so dreadfully and had forced her to do unspeakable things to her own sister. She moved herself closer to him.

'Remember me? Remember my sister, Khloe?' Her voice was clear but shaky. The man's eyes were possibly wider than they had ever been in his life. He managed grunting noises and what looked like a nod despite the vice holding his head. His tanned face oozed sweat and the muscles in his cheeks and neck quivered and twitched through two days of dark stubble.

'Remember us, Lombardi?' repeated Khloe. The girls had been introduced to him as Lombardi. He had assaulted and abused them as Lombardi, so now he would be punished as Lombardi. She removed the glass stopper from the sulphuric acid bottle.

The girls made a hesitant start on the restrained man. Kourtney moved the burner close enough to singe and shrivel the hairs on his legs while Khloe dripped a few drops of acid onto some folds of material on his oversized singlet. Fumes rose in the air and holes opened in the fabric.

The twins looked at each. Khloe nodded. Kourtney retrieved the leather cover and once again hid the guy's face.

'Better,' said Khloe.

'Much better,' added Kourtney.

The twins tried again. This time they burnt a small patch just below his knee and dripped acid onto his upper chest through the holes in his singlet. The man writhed and managed a high-pitched squeal around the sides of his gag. His muscles tightened and pushed against the restraints. Once again, the girls pulled back.

They put down the burner and the acid and held each other.

'We can't do this,' cried Kourtney.

'We just can't,' replied Khloe.

They went to the entry door, opened it and entered a small ante-room and kitchenette where Maxwell Judd stood sipping coffee. He didn't look like his usual self and had assumed the alter ego of "Joe", a long-haired weather-beaten man in his mid-fifties. Max was a genius at disguise and, using wigs, latex and make up, could transform his image to suit the occasion. He had at times worn masks or a balaclava but some of his customers had found this a little disconcerting, so these days, time permitting, he would assume a new identity. Doing so allowed him to remain anonymous and provided the level of security he needed.

'It's a difficult thing inflicting pain on another human being,' said *Joe* as he looked at the twins. 'Easier for some than others.'

'Is our mother around?' said Kourtney.

'We need to see her,' said Khloe.

'Karen!' called *Joe*. He sipped some more coffee.

Some footsteps clicked their way down the stairs to the underground bunker. A pair of silver high-heeled shoes came into view then the middle-aged lady appeared. She was dressed as if ready for a cocktail evening in a short, body-hugging silver dress which displayed ample cleavage. Her hair was long and blonde and fell in waves down her cheeks and onto her shoulders. She smiled, through caked on makeup, to the waiting three.

'We're sorry. We can't do it,' said the twins in unison. They both hugged their mother and sobbed. She stroked their heads, running her fingers through their hair.

'Don't you worry now. Please sit down here with Joe. He will make you both a nice warm drink. Kourtney, I'll need your apron. I have work to do.'

Karen kicked off her heels, put on the apron and smiled to the trio before entering the chamber. The door clicked shut.

*   *   *

At nine in the evening, after driving for an hour from his home at Oakdale, Max, still looking like Joe, pulled up on Old Bathurst Road about two hundred metres from the service station. This was the main road into Emu Plains, and there was very little going on. He waited a minute for a passing car to disappear then left his vehicle and moved slowly to the rear checking the surroundings as he went. Being just outside the residential area there was little to see – no nearby homes –no discernible activity. Across the road some dark silhouetted gums rocked gently in front of a low hanging half-moon. Max opened the rear doors of his black van with his gloved hands.

The body of a near-naked man was wrapped in thick plastic. What looked like his head protruded slightly from one end. He was still breathing but unconscious. All the hair on his head had been burnt off along with much of his scalp which was a weeping pulpy mess. His face had been eroded where acid had eaten away his flesh including his eyelids and one of his eyes. His nose and cheeks were stripped of any skin and there were several bright red bloody holes over his face big enough to put a finger in. Much of the plastic around his body clung to his red bleeding abdomen and legs. Karen Kearsley had unleashed fury.

Max picked him up, and holding him against his chest, carried him to the strip of grass beside the road, lay him down and turned him on his side.

On returning to his vehicle he threw his gloves in the back, pulled a mobile phone from his pocket and called triple zero.

Max gave all the location details and a false name. He reported that a man had been badly burnt and needed urgent help. After the call he pulled the phone to pieces. On the way home he threw the parts out the window.

CHAPTER 3

HOMELESS

It was the seventh of February and Maxwell Judd's forty-fourth birthday, as he painstakingly made his way around some of the one-hundred and twenty acres of his Oakdale property installing new motion detectors and several more discrete video surveillance cameras.

Despite it being a pleasant twenty-two degrees with a light breeze Max's bald head glistened with sweat in the morning sun. Treating outdoor tasks as a workout, running here and there, randomly dropping and doing twenty pushups, pulling himself up on branches, and lifting and relocating seemingly immovable large rocks was all part of keeping in shape.

His property was essentially divided into two areas. The front few acres devoted to the main home, gardens, large backyard shed and duck pond while the much larger rear area, separated from the home by bushland, a barbed wire fence and then an electric fence, was set aside for his work – such as it was. The underground concrete bunker, recently utilised by the Kearsley family, was beneath a garden shed, in a clearing, surrounded by acres of native bushland. Access was via a long gravel driveway from the rear of the block and through two security gates. It was this driveway and the area encircling the bunker that was the focus for the day.

For Max, the Oakdale home was not really a home anymore. A

home needed more than one occupant. And as grand, secure and well-equipped as it was, he really wanted Claire back. Maybe she would drop around unannounced for his birthday. He hadn't heard from her for over a month when she phoned to wish him a somewhat belated happy new year.

Following the traumas she had suffered at the hands of the now deceased Quentin Mortimer, Claire had left Max and moved in with her parents at St Leonards in Sydney. Although she had visited a few times it appeared she was not returning permanently any time soon. She was a big hit with Max's three children – Jenny, Tony and Ella, and had agreed to be there whenever they visited from Brisbane. So far this had been twice during the last two school holiday breaks.

Claire had dropped around on some other occasions saying she was checking on Max to see how he was managing, but Max had his doubts about her motivations as each time she left she took more of her belongings. A couple more of her brief visits and there would be nothing of hers left. To compound the matter, on the few times she had stayed overnight, she had slept in a separate bedroom. She was a strong woman both in mind and body but now she was broken. Being shot while protecting Max's children then only months later being kidnapped, tortured and stabbed can do that to a person. Max blamed himself entirely.

He knew the best way to get her back would be by making promises that, sooner or later, he would end up breaking. She wanted him to stop his pursuit of his son's killers and cease his efforts to help other victims achieve closure through hands-on-justice with the perpetrators. 'Get a real job, Max,' she had said, 'with proper pay and regular hours then we can have another look at our future.' Max couldn't do it. Not yet.

*   *   *

Max's son, Daniel, when aged only five years, had been sexually assaulted and murdered on the fifteenth of November 2013. There were three men involved. These three had been successfully identified via a snuff movie found by Max. It was one of hundreds of child porn videos owned by Walter James Robinson. Thanks mainly to Max, this notorious paedophile ringleader was now burning in hell for eternity.

Two of his son's murderers had been dealt with but there was one still outstanding – Charles Halliday, a business man and investor and part owner of some child care facilities. Max had seen him on TV a few months ago at the opening of a new centre but since then, despite many enquiries, surveillance, checking company records, phone directories, social media, taxation documents, electoral rolls and vehicle registrations the guy seemed invisible. His driver's licence was still registered to his old Victorian address. According to Max's sources at the customs department, it appeared that he had not left the country either. If his name popped up on a travel list Max was sure his contacts would be in touch.

It seemed Halliday had adopted a lifestyle not dissimilar to that of his own – staying out of the limelight, off social media, not using credit cards and perhaps using the names of others for his phone, car rego and residential address. No doubt he was aware of the death of his co-offender, Leonard Campbell – shot by police in 2013, and now the more recent disappearance of his colleague – Robert Mallory in 2017. He may have reason to think he could be on someone's radar, but it seemed unlikely, given the lengthy time period, that he would know exactly who, if anyone, was after him. It was possible that a private investigator or two may be trying to track the man who sexually assaulted their client's child. But to date, Halliday had never been charged or come to the attention of police in any state in the country. Max had the incriminating DVD from Robinson's collection. He, Claire, his counsellor Ian Friend, and more recently a trustworthy police detective were the only persons who knew it existed. Max was not even sure if Halliday knew about it. Robinson did many recordings with secret cameras. Whatever the case, Max had the evidence and it was his mission to find and rid the world of Charles Halliday.

*   *   *

He secured the final motion sensor for the day in the fork of a fifteen metre blue gum tree. The main branches were higher than the sensor and there was a clear area with only long grass around the base of the tree. It was an ideal spot. The sensor was wireless with a radius of twenty metres and a communication range to the base of five hundred metres and, being just one hundred metres from the bunker, would be perfect. The bunker would then relay any information to the monitoring room back in the house. Max marked the spot on his map. He could expect up to three years of battery life but regardless he had a schedule to change them all every twelve months.

He headed back to his black van then made the five kilometre trip down the gravel driveway, through the two gates, along an easement adjacent to his neighbour's land and back around to the front entrance. He parked in his garage between a white Camry sedan and a shiny Harley Davidson Road King.

*   *   *

All the buttons, lights and monitors in the hidden room appeared to be in operation. Max tilted back on a swivel office chair, put his hands around the back of his head, stretched and yawned.

'Happy Birthday, Max,' he grunted to himself. 'How is life treating you these days? Getting older but not much wiser it seems.' He let the chair tilt forward. 'It's a lonely thing this plotting and scheming.' He took out his mobile phone and placed it on the narrow bench. 'The retribution business is not conducive to making long lasting friendships. Maybe Max,' he told himself 'You should go on Tinder. How about …forty-four-year-old… no, thirty-nine-year-old male with a passion for torture and occasional killing seeks like-minded female to assist in dismembering and bloodletting… oh shit you're an idiot Max. It must be time to see the bloody counsellor again.' He slapped his hands on the bench. A glass full of a variety of pens bounced up slightly then toppled over.

He snatched up his phone and stabbed at a few buttons checking it was properly synced with his security system. As he held the device in his hand a Crosby Stills Nash and Young song began from another device — "*And you, of tender years, can't know the fears, that your elders grew by…*" Max's eyes lit up. This was his special phone —

the kids were calling for his birthday. His irritation evaporated.

CHAPTER 4

HAPPY BIRTHDAY

Chatting with his kids for thirty minutes was just the pick-me-up that Max needed. If nothing else happened on his birthday it wouldn't matter. His oldest, Jenny, at sixteen, was a bit of a worry and had broached the subject of getting Botox injections in her lips for her next birthday. A sum of two-thousand dollars had been mentioned. To temporarily avert world war three, Max had neither agreed nor disagreed. His son, Tony, was full of chat about soccer and his prowess as the under fourteen's new goalie. He was now following the English League – namely Nottingham Forest, and he was singing the praises for their pre-season victories in friendly games. Contrary to the older two, Ella was full of questions for her father asking about how his work was going, when he would be up to see them again and when would he be marrying Claire. The eight-year-old had asked three times during their vibrant conversation to speak with her. Max lied saying she was out back feeding the ducks.

With some reluctance, after finishing chatting with his kids, he had some words with Deb, his ex-wife. She barked on about the usual; wanting more money for the kids; reluctantly agreeing for the kids to fly down to see him next school holidays; overstating what a good parent her partner was.

'You are married to a millionaire, right?' said Max.

'Mark's financial status is completely irrelevant to this

conversation. As the kids get older expenses increase. I know you have been making regular contributions, but if you could put ten thousand in their account that would be a big help. Good schooling is important and can't be done on the cheap.'

'I'll do what I can,' conceded Max steering clear of an education debate.

'You do have regular and responsible employment now, don't you?' she squawked.

Max raised his eyebrows having heard nearly the same words from Claire not so long ago. 'I should think that as long as the money is arriving that should be of no concern to you. I am doing okay.'

'The kids come down to see you. I have agreed to give you some leeway here, Max. But you need to be an example. An employed, tax paying citizen and a good father.'

'Let's not do this, Deb.'

'Do what? Be responsible people? Trustworthy parents? Role models? I know you too well, Max.'

'For fuck's sake, Deb, it's my fucking birthday. Goodbye.' Max hung up as the words *Oh, Happy Birth…* left Deb's mouth. He lent back in his chair and did some slow breathing. She had pushed a few buttons, as per usual, but he was getting better at dealing with it. There were less anger outbursts and decreased periods of heightened anxiety. His sessions with his good friend and counsellor, Ian, were paying off.

A sharp high-pitched beep emanated from his phone. At the same time a red light flashed over the top of a monitor and the screen suddenly became brighter. It was Ted Horsley sauntering up the driveway with a hessian bag, no doubt filled with fresh produce. Ted lived next door. Not that next door was so close given the size of the properties, but Ted was fit enough for an old, partly retired farmer and could probably walk all day and night if he chose.

Max opened the front door before his neighbour had time to press the bell. The weathered face was slightly startled as his hand reached forward into empty space as the door opened ahead of him. 'Oh!'

'Hello Ted,' announced Max.

'Oh yes, you surprised me. Great timing.' He removed his tattered akubra.

'Saw you coming up the drive. What's up?'

'Nothing really. Some fine spuds, carrots and lettuce here.' Ted lifted the hessian bag up to Max. 'We have an abundance. Please take them. Norma says hi.'

Max took the bag. Ted's hands and fingernails were dirty. He had obviously just done some harvesting. Max stood looking down at the shorter man. Since moving in Ted had been around numerous times, always with vegies, always chatting and no amount of terse responding and declining of his offerings had made the slightest difference to his continued visits, enthusiasm and inquisitiveness.

'Beautiful weather, Max. One day after the other,' blurted Ted, feeling a little uncomfortable with the silence. 'Some showers tomorrow I'm thinkin'.'

'Do you want to come in?'

'What?' Ted's eyes widened, his head pulled back a little.

'You can come inside if you wish.'

'Are you sure?' He looked at his hands.

'Yeah. I'm sure. Come on. I'll show you to the bathroom.' Max stepped aside and beckoned him in.

It had been fifteen months since Max had moved to Oakdale and despite Ted's many visits he had never been invited inside. The two had chatted at the door and sat on the bench seat near the entrance. Max was not a fan of visitors so did his best to discourage them. But today was his birthday and he had seen enough of Ted to know he was a decent individual despite being a nosey bastard.

After cleaning up both men sat in the lounge on recliners drinking orange juice which was all Max had to offer. Ted had asked for a towel to sit on given his overalls were a little soiled. The two chatted about the weather, the Oakdale farmer's markets, the Aussie cricket team and even Prince Harry's forthcoming marriage to Meghan Markle. Ted prattled on about how well he was doing with the restoration of his Humber Super Snipe.

'Still needs some body work and reupholstering but I got her purrin' like a kitten now,' he smiled. The farmer looked about the room. 'Beautiful home, mate. Great painting, there.' The Fabian Perez painting "Man Smoking a Cigarette" was a standout feature mounted in the centre of the longer wall. He went quiet for a moment then looked at his socks and pushed his toes into the carpet before piping up with something more interesting.

'I haven't seen you driving that Monaro for some time.'

'I got rid of that ages ago,' replied Max immediately. 'Wasn't mine. Didn't know you had seen it.' He was slightly shocked but didn't show it. The Monaro had been left in his driveway months ago. It belonged to Quentin Mortimer, the dead snuff movie guy and son of the notorious Frank Mortimer. Frank had told Max he would track down his son's killer and the stolen Monaro. Until now he had heard nothing about the car. No news had been good news.

'I only saw it once,' continued Ted. 'By gees Max, you nearly ran me down. I was just coming into your driveway with some carrots and onions and you flew out onto the road. Nearly had a bloody heart attack, mate,' said Ted with a forced laugh. 'It was getting dark, but I thought it was red.'

'It was red and a well restored vehicle. It belonged to my nephew from the Gold Coast. He has it now,' lied Max. 'That was months ago.'

'May last year,' replied Ted promptly.

'And you bring it up now. Your brain puzzles me at times.'

'Norma says the same thing,' he quipped. 'Truth is, I had completely forgotten about it. Then I see this purple Monaro at the markets just back, and it got me thinkin' ya know. Was too loud. Huge exhaust pipes. Lots of noise.'

Max's phone let out two high-pitched beeps. He glanced at the screen which had a message - *Vehicle – area 1*.

'They can control and ruin your bloody life, those damn mobiles.'

'Yep. Message from a friend. Just coming up the driveway.'

'What's with this new generation. Couldn't wait thirty seconds to knock on the door, eh?'

'I guess not.'

'My daughter comes to see us. Barely gets off her damn phone. Can't talk to her anymore. Drives Norma bananas.'

Max stood. 'Excuse me a moment will you.' Ted nodded and raised the last of his juice. A moment later the doorbell chimed.

Max looked at the small monitor mounted on the wall not far from the entrance. It was Laura. She looked lovely in washed denim stretch jeans with torn knees and a fitting t-shirt with pink stripes. He smiled. She was one of only a handful who knew his address. It had taken him a while to trust her, but she was wonderful last year when Claire had been kidnapped. She had told him things that she probably shouldn't have, and their friendship had become stronger, even more so since Claire had moved away. He opened the door and let the detective in.

In the lounge Ted was already standing.

'Ted, this is Helen,' announced Max. 'A good friend of mine.' Laura lightly shook his hand, then gave Max a bemused glance.

'Nice to meet you, Ted,' she said.

'Likewise,' he tipped his head. 'Are you a local? I've not seen you around.'

'Helen is from Penrith,' said Max. 'We have some business to discuss.'

'Oh, of course. I was just on my way.' Ted dipped his head again. 'Goodbye then. Lovely to meet you, Helen.'

She nodded and smiled. 'Likewise,' she said.

Max escorted him to the door, grabbing the akubra on the way. 'Send my regards to Norma and thanks for the vegies.'

'Will do. Have a pleasant evening,' said Ted with a raise of his eyebrows. 'Nice looking lady by the way.'

'Goodbye, Ted.' Max closed the door and watched him through the peephole as he wandered down the long driveway. As he left the property Max's phone beeped twice. The message said – *Person - area 1.*

Back in the lounge Max and Laura hugged. He kissed her on the cheek.

'Helen? Penrith?' said Laura. Her hands touched his bare shoulders, ran down his sleeveless t-shirt and parked on his hips.

'The less he knows the better. You know me. Just being careful.'

'Yeah, I know too well.' She took her hands off him and picked up a small paper bag from the sofa. Max took hold of the string handle. 'Happy birthday!' She popped up on her toes and pecked him on the cheek then dropped onto the sofa and patted the cushion next to her. Max sat and peered into the bag.

He lifted out a magnetic GPS tracking device about the size of a small coffee mug.

'This is a first.'

'I thought it may be useful in your *line of work*,' said Laura. 'Has a battery life of one-hundred and twenty hours. Connects easily to your mobile phone. Attaches securely and discretely to most vehicles within thirty seconds.'

'Wow!' He looked at her. She had a big relaxed smile. Her green eyes and freckles seemed to be accentuated. His phone beeped twice – *Vehicle – area 1.*

'Looks like I'm winning the popular vote this evening!' Again, he moved towards the monitor on his way to the front door. A white Toyota Prius pulled up behind Laura's Hyundai i30. Claire walked around the Hyundai, running her fingers over the bonnet and peering through the windows before making her way to the front of the house. This evening she was wearing a grey sports bra with a black border, long black tights and her Nikes. She always looked so good in her active wear. She knew Max liked it.

He took a deep breath and muttered *Fuck,* softly through gritted teeth, then opened the door.

'Hello honey,' he smiled broadly. 'Lovely to see you.'

'Hi Max, happy birthday.' She pecked him on the lips and handed him a parcel. 'You have visitors?'

'Thanks so much. Yes, yes. I do have a visitor,' said Max. Claire was quickly past him and into the foyer.

'In the lounge,' said Max. He pushed a hand over his face and across the top of his bald head before falling in behind her.

'You've met Laura once or twice I think,' he said as he caught her up. Laura stood and extended her hand. The two ladies shook lightly.

'Hello Claire,' said Laura warmly. 'Nice to see you.'

Claire just nodded and pushed out a smile.

'Why don't we all sit down. I can grab a drink or two,' said Max.

'No thanks, Max. I was just about to leave anyway,' said Laura. 'I'm sure you and Claire have some catching up to do. I can see myself out. Some other time Claire,' she smiled and moved past her. 'Have a happy birthday,' she looked at Max touched his shoulder lightly, winked and left. The front door opened then clicked shut.

'She didn't need to leave on my account,' said Claire.

'She had another engagement this evening and was about to go,' lied Max as dismissively as he could. There was potential trouble here and it was almost palpable. Max felt the gun was being loaded when she checked Laura's Hyundai. Then the hair trigger was set when she entered the lounge. She sat on the sofa. Max dropped onto the other end with his parcel and proceeded to unwrap it.

Claire picked up the paper bag and looked at the tag. '*Happy birthday, Max. Love Laura,*' she said with a head tilt. 'That seems very friendly then.'

'Yes, she's a nice lady,' he opened the parcel and feigned as much excitement as he could muster. 'Thanks so much. Brut is my favourite and I was low on supplies.' He wasn't convincing. The phone beeped twice as Laura drove away.

'There she goes,' said Claire.

'All systems working fine here. It's a very secure home. Thanks so much for this.' He held up the Brut box with deodorant and cologne.

'It's not quite a Magnetic GPS Vehicle Tracker. How much do these things cost? What else did she give you for your birthday?' The finger was on the trigger.

'They're not so dear these days. There were no other gifts,' said Max.

'Hmm… Really?'

'Come on now. She is just a friend. That's it… how's your mum and dad?'

'*Love Laura* – it says on the gift card.'

'There's love and there's love, you know. She'd only been here five minutes.'

'Okay, so if she'd been here longer…'

'No, honestly Claire, it's not that sort of relationship.' Max raised both hands like a stop sign. 'We're good friends and colleagues. You are the one for me. I want you with me. Living here, sharing everything. No one else. My Claire. And only my Claire.' He moved closer to her. 'Max and Claire that's the way it should be. I love you so very much. I struggle without you.'

She put down the GPS and wriggled a little closer. Max was now out of the gun sights. They leaned in and kissed briefly on the lips then Claire pulled back.

'I'm thinking of selling the Pelican Street unit?' she announced.

'What? No, please.' Max shook his head.

'You'll get half.'

'I don't want half. I still use that place. I need it,' he pleaded.

Claire had sold her apartment in Melbourne before they left, and with a contribution from Max they had purchased the Surry Hills unit in Claire's name.

'I'll need a place of my own one day,' said Claire.

'But you already have a place. Here. With me.'

'You know my terms with that deal. And I can't live at Pelican Street ever again. Just collecting my clothes from there sent shivers down my spine. I can't become a target to some crazed or perverted psychopath with a vendetta against you. Not again. I even get worried at my parent's place, thinking someone is watching and plotting something – some way to hurt me, or even Mum and Dad.'

'You're still seeing a therapist, right?'

'Naturally. What about you? Still seeing Ian?'

'I am. Next week.'

'Maybe he can buy me out and then gift it to you? Tell me this, Max. Is he a bottomless pit of cash? He has given you so much. Just seems a bit weird to me. I have never ever known anyone like that. He spends over a million bucks on this place, then seventy-grand more on security work Spends another hundred and fifty on the bunker. Buys you vehicles. Spots you more cash from time to time. And all you pay is utilities and rates. Really?'

'I do earn my own money too you know,' said Max indignantly.

'Your job security is a little flimsy to say the least.'

'Ian is a good friend. Done well with property over the years. We share similar interests and, as you know, he sends me referrals.'

'Oh yes, I know that only too well. You end up meeting some right charmers.'

Max opened his hands and glanced around. 'And you know what I say about this place.'

'Yes, yes. Right here is the safest place on the planet. I know.

But I can't be holed up here twenty-four seven.'

Then the doorbell chimed and instantly Max was on his feet. He looked at his phone. No beeps. No messages. 'Stay right where you are. I'll go check.'

'Max!' she squawked, detecting a hint of urgency in Max's voice and putting a hand to her chest.

'Don't move. I've got this.'

Max looked at the monitor. A slender hairless young man in old running shoes, wearing shorts and a white t-shirt that was at least three sizes too big, stood there with a stern expression. Max opened the door.

'Ezekiel! Oh my God!' Max wanted to grab him in a big bear hug but knew better. The young man was very sensitive to close body contact. He took his hand with both of his and shook it.

'It's Jeremiah.'

'What?'

'My name is no longer Ezekiel Kaufman it's Jeremiah Cornelius.' The young man prised Max's grip from his hand and arm.

'Honey,' shouted Max turning his head back. 'Everything's okay. You can relax.'

'How did you get to my door?'

'I walked.'

'But no alarms were triggered.'

'I walked carefully. Guided by God.'

'Yes, I should've known,' nodded Max excitedly. 'Come in. Come in. Please.'

Jeremiah entered the foyer just as Claire did from the other end.

'Hello Claire,' he said.

Claire gasped and covered her mouth. Tried to scream but just made gagging sounds. Her face drained to white. She became limp as a wet washcloth and collapsed to the floor.

*　　　　*　　　　*

It was ten minutes later when she woke up – lying on the sofa with Max wiping her forehead. Most of the colour had returned to her face. She stirred and open and closed her eyes a few times. A second later she regained her orientation.

'Is he here? Where is he?' She tried to sit up and look around.

'Hey, it's okay. There is no danger.' Max gently pushed her head back onto the cushion.

'It was him. Ezekiel. Wasn't it?'

'Yes. But he's one of the good guys. He saved your life. He's in another room.'

'I must leave. Go home. Now.'

'Sure. But in twenty minutes or so. When I am happy you are okay to drive.'

Claire didn't need reminding that Ezekiel saved her life and she didn't need reminding of the whole incident. The one and only time she had seen him was when he tore out Quentin Mortimer's throat with his teeth, then moved his blood-soaked face near her and pulled a knife from her shoulder.

Thirty minutes later Claire drove away. Any chance of a return visit seemed light years away.

*   *   *

Max wandered back through the foyer, the hallway, the lounge and another hallway to a spare bedroom. He could see the light on under the door. He knocked and opened the door. Jeremiah was standing upright, head bowed and holding a Bible in front of his chest. It was a basic bedroom with single bed, built in wardrobe, bedside table with lamp and one window with external metal bars. There were no electronic monitors present.

The young man softly recited scripture for a few more seconds then looked up at Max. 'The outcome for your birthday is no doubt somewhat different than you expected.'

'What are you up to, Ezekiel?'

'It's Jeremiah. And I am reading the Bible.'

'What are you really up to? Why are you here?'

'Am I not welcome?'

'You are very welcome. And I am pleased to see you looking quite well. For some reason I like you despite your unusual way of going about your business.'

The two bald men sat together on the bed. One looking strong as an ox and the other thin and gaunt, a look that belied his true strength.

'Claire is a good person. She suffers for you, Max.'

'She suffers because of me. And you scared her half to death.'

'She does not fear me. She's fears her own memory. She fears for her future and for you.'

Max turned his head to the side and just stared. Once again

captivated by the unusual man.

'If you would prefer, I would be happy to reside once more in your underground accommodation,' continued Jeremiah.

'No,' smiled Max. 'That won't be necessary. But there will need to be a few rules for however long you choose to remain here.'

'I understand, Max. I will return to this room and remain here whenever anyone visits. If you leave the premises, I understand you will arm the house and once again I will remain here until you return.'

'Have you been working on your psychic abilities since I last saw you?'

'I am aware of what is necessary for you. This is simply the most logical option.'

'Once again, why are you here?'

'I believe the Lord will make that clear to me in due course,' said Jeremiah. He raised his head to the ceiling and slowly stood. With his arms raised towards the roof he said, 'I will not put thee to death, neither will I give thee into the hand of these men that seek thy life.' He sat again.

'Shit! What's that all about?'

'Words of the Lord from the book of Jeremiah. I am not yet fully aware of their context.'

Max stood. 'Look, help yourself to anything in the kitchen. Use the facilities as you wish. If you have any more premonitions or spiritual enlightenments, please let me know. I do have some more questions for you. Right now, though, I need to chill for a few minutes.'

'Thank you, Max. You will find some meditation helpful.'

Max grunted and left the room.

CHAPTER 5

YOGI GOES FISHING

Thanks to methamphetamine, cocaine and to a lesser extent a few other illegal affiliations, Frank Mortimer was a wealthy man. His importation supply pipelines from South America through the north island of New Zealand for cocaine, and from China through Thailand and Indonesia for meth had been very lucrative and with only one major seizure of product in the past ten years. Generally, it was fishing trawlers that completed the last leg of the journey. Sometimes other vessels and sea planes had proved successful and they were always a good backup, especially after a tip off. Now and then, some owners of private yachts, unbeknown to them, would bring in major quantities of drugs.

The "More-t'-Moor", Frank's luxury cruiser, was anchored at Grotto Point not far from Castle Rock Beach and near the entrance to Sydney Harbour. Every minute or so, at the rear of the vessel on the swim platform, Diego scooped burly from a bucket with a soup ladle and tossed it in a wide arc into the water. Diego was a man of few words, and the way he looked he seldom needed them, with his body builder physique speaking for itself. The white t-shirt and short shorts looked as though they could split at any moment with just one flex – a splash of green and Hollywood would be signing him up for the next sequel. The "hulkish" squareness of his head was further emphasised by a short cut shave on both sides.

Frank had positioned himself upwind from Diego on the deck above and behind the swim platform. At his back was the stern cockpit and the entry to the well-appointed living area. Nevertheless, the foul odour occasionally managed to find his nostrils requiring him to cover his nose with his hand and shake his head.

From behind him appeared another man. Eli Christiansen was another bouncer of Frank's, but also the skipper of the vessel and a half decent cook. He had taken over when Ronnie retired several months ago. The skipper had excellent credentials both for catering, navigation and busting heads which made him perfect for the job. From the neck down he was similarly built to Diego but without the tight apparel. He was a man that needed to shave twice a day, although there was a scar on the right side of his chin that never grew any hair at all and always looked prominent eight hours post shave. Eli removed his skipper's cap and moved alongside Frank.

'Fuck, this is a disgusting business at times, Eli,' said the curly haired business man.

'Yes, sir. Can I get you something to drink sir?

'Come on, Eli. When will you stop calling me sir? You know you can call me Frank.'

'Yes, Sir Frank,' replied the skipper. 'A drink?'

'No.' He waved him away. Eli tipped his head, put his cap back on and left.

'What do you think, Yogi?' he shouted. 'Pretty nasty business this!'

On the swim platform a couple of metres from Diego was a thin man secured to an aluminium outdoor chair. His legs were heavily taped to those of the chair. His arms were similarly attached to each of the chair arms. There was an abundance of tape around his upper chest, extending around the back of the seat. The chair was only a few centimetres from the edge of the platform, and while he could possibly rock it around a little, it seemed inadvisable to do so. The man's only clothing was a pair of briefs. This was Yogi, a somewhat emaciated man with a weathered complexion, pointy features and an unshaven face. He was thirty-eight years old but by appearance could have been twice that.

'Come on Frank. I would never do anything to harm your business. I really wouldn't. I respect you Frank,' quivered Yogi.

'Yet when you found out that I was looking for you, you went into hiding and quite successfully for a while,' said Frank. 'Why would you do that I wonder?'

'I was worried, scared. I was petrified that other people had given you the wrong information. And that's what has happened, Frank. You have been misinformed. Please, I am not your enemy. I respect you. And, quite honestly, I fear you. No way would I cross you. Not a chance.' Yogi strained his head turning back trying to see the drug king.

'Really,' replied Frank through a handkerchief held over his nose. He took a moment then pushed the hanky back into his pocket. 'It seems to me that stupid people will do stupid things. Dumb people make dumb decisions. Short term thinkers live short term lives.'

Diego flung out the contents of another ladle into the water.

There was a swirl and a splash of something moving quickly just below the surface. It caught Yogi's attention and his eyes widened. He managed to jump the chair a couple of centimetres further way from the edge.

'Careful my friend. That platform can get slippery and the chair is not particularly stable,' smiled Frank.

'I will help you, Frank,' quivered Yogi. 'I'll ask around, get information, find out who is behind all this.'

'Do you know who murdered my son?'

'I don't. But I will make it my mission to find out.'

'It was very brutal…'

Frank Mortimer's son, Quentin, was murdered in what appeared to be a drug related hit. His throat was ripped apart and shards of the drug ICE were scattered all over the floor and around his body. Frank was not overly distressed by the loss of Quentin, given his son's predilection for torture, sexual abuse and the making of snuff movies. However, blood is thicker than water, and Frank wanted payback. He also wanted the return of his classic Holden Monaro which was stolen at the time of the killing.

'My son was not a good person,' continued Frank. 'But he was my son, and someone will be paying for his demise. You have a chance here to convince me of two things. One, you had no connection in any way with his death or the drugs, and two, you can genuinely provide me with assistance in resolving this matter.'

Frank reclined in his chair and helped himself to a piece of apple which was on the cheese and fruit platter next to him.

'I am not a killer. Quentin was someone who I would go out of my way to avoid seeing. I knew of his reputation.'

Frank crunched away on his apple as he scooped up some blue cheese on a cracker.

'There was some guy...' said Yogi hesitantly. 'A rich guy. Sent some lowlife junkies to see me with some story of getting me workin' for him. I was never about to do that, Frank. You are the man and that's that. Then those junkies ripped off my shit...'

'Who's shit?' blurted Frank.

'Sorry Frank. Yes. Yours. They ripped off your shit. There was an explosion in the back room. Lots of smoke. When it cleared the junkies were gone with your K of crystal.'

'You should take better care of property that is given to you in good faith.'

'I know. I'll make it up to you. I will. For sure.'

'We had a good thing going there, Yogi. I trusted you. Then, the first time I go the extra mile, you fuck me over.'

'I will make it right. Work for free, Frank. Anything.'

Frank looked at Diego and gave him a nod and a smile through a mouthful of cheese. The big man put the ladle back in the bucket and somehow squeezed out a box cutter from his tight shorts.

'Fuck it, Frank!' squealed Yogi at the sight of the blade. Diego strode over to him and without hesitation made three long cuts down the lower part of his chest to his abdomen, avoiding the binding tape. The cuts were each about a centimetre deep. The flesh parted neatly like butter on a hot knife, blood filled the wound then flowed freely, quickly seeping into Yogi's white cotton underwear.

'Noooo!' he squealed. 'Frank, please! I can find this guy. Work undercover for you. We can nail him. You and me. A team, Frank. Please.' Yogi's frantic gaze shifted between trying to see Frank and then Diego.

'His name?' asked Frank calmly.

'If I knew I would tell you. Shit! But I'll find out. I have contacts. I can do this for you. I can help, Frank.'

'The bull sharks are quite prolific around here. Looks like there is at least four out there.'

'You don't need to do this,' pleaded Yogi. A huge splash only a metre from the swim platform caught everyone's attention. 'Fuck!' shouted Yogi. Blood was dripping from his underwear onto the platform and flowing over the side into the water.

'Okay Yogi. I think we can release you from that chair now,' said Frank with his usual relaxed smile.

Yogi took a deep breath and sighed in a moment of relief from his terror. Frank nodded to Diego. The body builder stepped over to the captive and took a firm hold of his taped forearms.

'You can just rip that tape away now,' panted Yogi. 'Thank you, Diego.' He looked at the unchanged face of the hulk then back at the grip on his arms. 'Come on, man. There's a good chap. Rip away. You can do it.' Then the chair rose in the air, the two men's noses almost touched. Diego catapulted it, with its contents, into the sea.

A wide-eyed Yogi went down head first as the chair arced over in a semi-circle. The splash stifled a scream that had only just begun.

Yogi sank momentarily before his taped legs bobbed back up. The water became alive with thrashing and splashing, turning red. The chair and its occupant descended.

'I venture to say, that was not quite the way he expected to be released.' Frank helped himself to some more fruit.

Eli arrived with more cheese. 'It seems the wildlife have quite an appetite around here,' he said as he added the cheese to the platter. 'This King Island Ash Brie is superb, Sir Frank.'

'Diego, come and try this kiwi fruit. It is delicious.' He waved him over. 'Eli, take a seat, have a feed and enjoy the scenery.'

CHAPTER 6

KLONG PREM CENTRAL

Charles considered his three-piece, deep-blue wool suit the perfect business accessory. Custom designed and tailored, it was a perfect fit, and the forty-five-year-old looked stunningly handsome as he sat in a lounge chair reading a fitness magazine.

In front of him, on a large coffee table, was a cheese platter and a cappuccino. The Thai Airways business lounge had all the facilities necessary to keep the most finicky travelers happy. Halliday had arrived early to take full advantage of the service and get the most out of his business class ticket.

It was to be a short trip – fly out Tuesday, fly home Thursday with carry-on luggage only. Today's flight left in an hour, at midday, and would touch down at Bangkok's Suvarnabhumi Airport around nine and a half hours later at the local time of five-thirty in the evening. He was booked into a Superior Room at the Novotel Suvarnabhumi Airport Hotel. There would only be three places he would be visiting – the airport, the hotel and Klong Prem Central Prison.

Apart from his Australian money, Halliday had 6 five-hundred Baht notes – equal to about one-hundred and thirty Australian dollars. That would be more than enough for his outing on Wednesday morning.

He had booked the flight as late as he could. It was possible someone may be trying to monitor his activities, and if they were well connected, this trip may send up a red flag. This was not a big deal on the departure, but considerable care would need to be taken when he returned to Sydney and left the airport. If everything went as expected he would be better placed to deal with any potential threats following his Thailand visit. While there was some risk, it was calculated and manageable.

*   *   *

The flight was comfortable and the service impeccable with the Boeing 747-400 landing at exactly five-thirty as expected. Charles Halliday had checked in to the Novotel, enjoyed a couple of cocktails in the Atrium Lounge and now, at eight o'clock, was in the hotel's Sala Thai Restaurant enjoying the Spicy and Sour Asian Red Tail Cat Fish Soup.

It was good to have money and Charles liked spending it. He had made some rewarding business decisions buying, selling and operating child care facilities around the country. For the most part he preferred his own company, occasionally catching up with business associates as the need arose. Never though, at his own home. At their place or office, at coffee shops or restaurants and now and then at conferences.

When at home there was no wife, no kids and no pets. His home was beautifully furnished and well-appointed inside, but outside was nothing special, a low-set regular suburban brick and timber house in a quiet street. Nothing to attract unwanted attention. On one side was a vacant allotment, on the other an easement and with a park at the back it was ideal. It was a rental house with the owner overseas and not likely to be back anytime soon or even at all. A private rental arrangement had been organised by a helpful friend, no agents, no real estates, and it was possible he may even acquire the property himself if everything went according to plan. Until such time as he secured a legitimate alternative identity, he would stay where he was and keep off any government and real estate records.

From time to time he would like to enjoy the company of younger people and for that he had five motels and two hotels he would use. For each place he would dress down, wear glasses, use a specific alias for each location and always pay cash.

*   *   *

On Wednesday morning Charles had a light breakfast delivered to his room. He changed into jeans, a casual red check button up shirt and a pair of sandals. At ten-thirty he hopped into the yellow and green taxi to set off on the forty-two-kilometre journey to Klong Prem Central Prison. His visit had been booked and approved two weeks ago. He was permitted only twenty minutes – more than enough time.

The taxi driver was a middle-aged man with a round, permanently smiling face and excess girth. The taxi was decorated with a plethora of colourful Buddhist symbols. Some mounted on the dashboard and many others hanging from the rear-view mirror like Christmas decorations on a tree. Even the inside roof was adorned with posters and drawings.

'Klong Prem Central Prison,' announced Charles as he entered the vehicle. The smiling driver nodded as the vehicle departed.

'You tourist?' he asked.

'Ah ha,' said Halliday not wishing to discuss the real purpose of his trip.

'You see drug dealer?'

'Yes,' lied Halliday.

'Many tourists go. Visit drug men. Talk. Buy them smokes, food.'

'I'll be doing the same. Should be interesting.'

'Not see murderers or sex men,' said the driver shaking his head and trying to frown over his smile.

'No way.'

'You like me play music?'

'Sure.'

He pushed a CD into the player. A moment later Katy Perry was singing "Waking up in Vegas". Halliday raised his eyebrows. The driver tapped his fingers and at times completely let go of the steering wheel to clap his hands together and push them in the air to the tune while rocking about in his seat. As the fifth song, "I Kissed a Girl", came to an end they turned into the entrance of the prison grounds.

The car moved slowly around a massive roundabout and pulled up in front of an aged, long two-story building, behind which was a much taller guard outpost looking like an air traffic control tower. Charles gave the driver five-hundred Baht for a fare of four-hundred and fifty Baht, showed him two more notes and asked him to wait. 'Yes please,' he happily nodded.

Klong Prem Central Prison was massive and could hold up to twenty-thousand prisoners in several compounds. Today Halliday was going to the men's section for men with sentences under twenty-five years. This area held just over six thousand inmates.

He joined a short queue of four in front of a window with horizontal metal bars and a recessed metal tray on which items could be exchanged. Looking around he tipped his head and smiled to the three armed guards who didn't seem inclined to smile back.

'Papers and ID,' said the uniformed man behind the window. Charles handed over his approval letter and passport. The man quickly inspected the document then looked at the passport and back at him twice.

'Very good. You fill out this now,' he pushed through a form together with the approval letter and passport. 'Over there at the bench. Then come back.'

'Thank you very much,' said Charles warmly and giving a slight bow. At the bench he completed the form which seemed much like a repeat of his approval letter. Name; date of birth; home address; Thailand address (if international visitor); passport number and place of issue; name of inmate; reason for visit; relationship to inmate; tick if purchasing canteen items for inmate; date of last visit (if applicable); Sign and date. He completed the form saying he was a cousin and returned it to the window-man who thanked him, gave him a ticket, and directed him to proceed down the corridor.

Four more security staff were equipped with hand held metal detectors and were providing plastic trays for visitors. Two of the three visitors ahead of him placed their mobile phones in the trays which were labelled with the appropriate ticket number and slid into a large slotted trolley. A guard stood in front of the third visitor, a large man wearing a cowboy hat, and tapped his detector against his oversized belt and buckle.

'In tray please,' said the guard politely.

The man shook his head. 'I prefer my trousers to stay up if you don't mind, sir.' The man laughed at his own little joke while looking around for approval or a smile from others.

'In tray please,' repeated the guard more firmly.

'Not happenin' bud,' he replied with a south American drawl.

'Not in tray. No visit. You hold pants up.'

'No. Now go on, you just let me through.' He tried to squeeze past the guard. A big mistake. In a flash two M16 assault rifles were pointing at him.

'Hold up there, guys.' He raised his arms. 'Didn't know you were that serious.'

'You leave now,' said the first guard. 'No visit allowed.'

'Now hold on there one doggone minute.' Another two guards grabbed his upper arms. 'I don't need to be man handled,' he bellowed. With one armed guard following they escorted him from the building.

Charles was next. The guard scanned him and found nothing.

'No phone?'

'Left it at the hotel,' said Charles. 'You're doing a fine job here. Thank you for keeping everyone safe.'

'Yes, sir. Very good sir,' smiled the guard. 'You continue now.'

*   *   *

Halliday arrived at a very long tiled area outside a wall of heavy square wire mesh in front of the visiting section. There was a long row of at least thirty identical stools each in front of a pale blue bench. Clear Perspex partitions separated each area and there was a phone in front of each stool. Many visitors, mostly women, were already chatting to inmates via the telephones.

He was directed to a stool. He sat and picked up the phone. Between where the inmates sat, and the row of visitors, was a corridor where guards could wander back and forth.

As Halliday looked ahead through the squares of wire, he saw a forlorn looking Ross Miller sit and pick up the phone.

It was at least three years since he had seen him. Back in Melbourne, when Miller was a police detective, they had caught up a few times and shared some information. He was a tall fit man back then. Now, though no less tall, he was thin with prominent cheek bones and looked unwell. The past two years in this overcrowded hell had taken its toll. His sad looking expression was nothing particularly new, he always looked like that.

'Hey,' grunted Miller into the receiver.

'Hey. You look like shit,' replied Halliday.

'Shit would be an improvement.'

'You seen a doctor?'

'Twice.'

Miller went on to describe the living conditions. Sleeping on cement with only a blanket, always being in contact with those lying around you and bathing using a ladle out of a cement trough.

He had been beaten a few times. At first, he could stick up for himself, but as time went by, he had become less able to do so. Giardia had plagued him for the past six months with frequent abdominal cramps, vomiting and diarrhoea.

'What's happening with you? How's business?' asked a disinterested Miller.

'Business is great. I'm making good money. Can't complain.'

'Okay… so how's your *other* business?'

'Ah yeah.' Charles paused a moment. 'Let's say there are a few struggling families that need some extra money. Happy to help them out where I can. Overall, it is a little slower than I would like.'

Miller nodded his understanding and forced a half grin. 'You're not here for a social call. What's going on?'

'You remember Leonard Campbell was shot in 2013?'

'Of course, I remember.'

'Now Bob Mallory has vanished. Looks like he was abducted and murdered. We all did a few gigs together.'

'Yeah. What else?' asked Miller.

'He was taken by a tall strong guy with a squarish jaw. Had blonde locks and a goatee. This guy had some morals. Had a chance to fuck this pretty gym instructor but didn't.'

'I'll bet any phone number no longer works.'

'Correct.'

'Mallory's laptop is gone. Cops took his phone.'

'I have to ask,' said Miller 'Did you ever do a number ten with those two guys, Campbell and Mallory?' Charles Halliday stared at him, his eyes a little wider. Then he glanced side to side. No one seemed to be paying them much interest, so he just nodded. 'Okay,' continued the ex-detective. 'Did WJR have any involvement?'

'Shit, that was back in 2013!' said Halliday. 'WJR made all the arrangements. He insisted on doing so.'

'Then he made a movie.'

'He promised he wouldn't do that.'

'A number ten!' Miller almost shouted then looked around checking he hadn't attracted attention. 'You kiddin',' he said softly. 'He wouldn't miss a chance like that. So, are we talkin' a number ten with the initial of D?'

'That sounds about right.'

'Then you are in deep shit,' said Miller with a wide-eyed nod. 'Deeper shit than me.'

'Really? You think it's that guy? And he's now in Sydney?'

'Yeah, the same guy that orchestrated my occupancy in this shithole... Maxwell Judd. Ex-cop from Melbourne. And forget the blonde hair and goatee. This guy is a master of disguise. And he's well connected and invisible. He has an ex-wife and kids in Brisbane and some girlfriend that's a teacher. Her name is... fuck... Clara maybe...can't recall exactly, but something like that.'

'Maxwell Judd, after all this time.'

'He is relentless,' said Miller.

'I remember his name. He's the cop that shot Campbell. At the time I thought that was the end of it – case closed.'

'I can give you a couple of names in the force. They are onside. Could possibly help with Judd and maybe a few introductions. You're getting some canteen stuff for me, right?'

'For sure. Yes.'

'And I want smokes. Not that I smoke, but they're good currency in here.'

Miller listed a few other items he wanted and got Halliday's agreement before giving him the two names and the contact details as best he could remember.

A guard came over to Halliday.'

'That's it. You finish now.'

'You nail this prick,' added Miller quickly. 'And as you take him down say hello from me.'

Halliday put the phone down and gave him a thumbs up.

CHAPTER 7

THERAPY

Max found himself back in a familiar setting. On the black leather chaise lounge in Ian Friend's office at Hastings Psychology in Sydney. Ian was currently discussing a case with a colleague in the adjoining office and promised to be only a few minutes.

There were a couple of concerning thoughts running through Max's mind that he just couldn't shake. The whole matter with the then named Ezekiel, and how it all unfolded almost as if scripted in some way. And all this initiated by his conversation with his therapist, Ian. Max had asked him three times over past months if the young man had ever turned up to see him. This was a reasonable question seeing Ezekiel had agreed to do so when the two met in the psych ward at Gosford. The counsellor had repeatedly denied ever seeing him again. Stuck in his mind too were Claire's recent words about Ian's money and unusual generosity. It was something Max had never really considered before. After all the guy charges three-hundred dollars or more an hour, does consulting work and makes money on property. He can afford to be generous. They have been friends for so long and they both have a similar mind set on what is real justice. Surely this is all very reasonable, Max told himself.

Ian was taking longer than expected so Max got up and wandered around the spacious room. There were the two beautiful recliners for less formal chats, a bookcase with all manner of psychology and psychiatry books, a small sink set into a wood grain bench unit, and near the window, a desk with all the regular office bits and pieces and a computer.

Max moved the curtains aside and peered down from the fourth floor into busy Elizabeth Street. It was a top location right across from Hyde park. The Wednesday lunch crowd were scurrying about almost impatiently, probably a byproduct of thirty-minute meal breaks. He wondered if we could learn something from the Greeks and Spaniards.

Just as his thoughts flicked back to Ian's wealth, one of his three phones vibrated in the front left pocket of his jeans. The display read, *Neil K.*

'Been a while, Rusty,' answered Max.

'Too long, mate. How's the new lady?'

'Estranged.'

'Fuck, sorry.'

'Hopefully a short-term thing. What's happening?'

'Got a hit, mate. Charles Halliday left for Bangkok with Thai Airways yesterday at noon. Booked on return flight tomorrow. Flight THA113 arriving at seven in the evening.'

'Yes, that's great news.' Max clenched a fist and punched the air. 'Did you see any listed address?'

'There are no addresses on passports, but on file we have a residential address at Kingsford, and a post box for his postal address. I'll text them to you.'

'Much appreciated.'

The door opened and Ian Friend entered. 'Back at last, Max.' He closed the door, turned and noticed him near the window on the phone. 'Sorry.' He raised a hand. 'I can give you a few more minutes.'

'It's okay,' said Max. 'Rusty, gotta go. Take care and thank you. I'll be in touch again soon. We'll catch up and share a fruit juice somewhere.'

'Or maybe a lager or two.'

'You never know. Bye.' Max cut the call. A moment later a text came through with the addresses. He changed his mind about the chaise lounge and dropped into the recliner.

'Okay,' said Ian. 'No in-depth analysis, today.' He sat in the other.

'We'll see.'

'Sorry I didn't get to come over the other day. Had an urgent late consult at The Sydney Clinic. How was your birthday?'

'Probably just as well you didn't,' replied Max. 'A crowd was gathering, and a storm was brewing.'

'If I had to guess Claire was there and Deb called you.'

'Not bad old fella, but slightly worse. Deb had called earlier with the kids. Laura visited and then Claire rocked up.'

'Ah... tricky... tense,' he replied with a nod. They looked at each other. Ian's big blue eyes on his soft round face were full on in counselling mode. Max had seen him enough times, and he had that look that made you feel so relaxed and comfortable that you could happily blurt out every sin and problem you ever had in your life. There was the visit of Ezekiel/Jeremiah. Max decided not to say anything about that.

'There's something else,' continued Ian, almost posing a question.

Max swallowed. 'There always is.'

'*You're* a bit pale. Don't *mind* me. I *will* get you a water.' The counsellor's subtle emphasis on key words was almost imperceptible. He stood and went to the wood bench not waiting for a response. 'Just *relax.*' He opened a door to reveal a small fridge and shelves with cups, glasses, a few small plates, coffee and tea sachets, individual biscuits in plastic packets and a few assorted sweets. 'Can I *open up* a biscuit for you?'

Max shook his head. 'Water will be fine.'

'*And tell me* what particular *things* Laura had to say?'

Max looked at Ian. The question somehow seemed a little odd and out of place. Maybe he was feeling a bit light-headed after all. Ian took two glasses and a carafe of cold water from the fridge.

'Huh?' muttered Max.

Ian placed the glasses on the coffee table and filled them.

'Thanks.'

Ian took his glass and lay back in the recliner. He drank then took a few deep breaths. A moment later Max found himself doing the same. Then he smiled.

'What's troubling you?' asked Ian. 'And something seems slightly amusing.'

'Yes, I get it now. You nearly got me, you bastard. The old Jedi mind control. You taught me that. You nearly sucked me in.'

Ian laughed. 'Next time I will.' They both laughed.

'My neighbour dropped around as well. He left when Laura turned up. Laura left when Claire turned up.' He hoped revealing this other visit would be enough to placate his mind reading friend.

'When did Claire leave?'

Very clever thought Max. He managed to restrain himself from blurting out Ezekiel. 'She didn't stay over which was disappointing. Dropped off a small gift. We chatted about her moving back but it was a conversation that went nowhere.'

'And how are you going for cash these days?'

Well, there it was, the perfect opening. Now how to tackle it without being too nosey or offensive. 'I received a little from Mrs Kearsley. I'm getting by. Why, are you offering me a loan?'

'Always happy to donate to a good cause, Max. You have a job to do and there seems to be regular clientele that need assistance.'

'Gee-whiz mate, you bought the land and house, paid for the upgrades and the bunker. You set me up when I was in Melbourne. I know you earn good money, but hell did you win the lotto or something?'

'Property buys and sells have been favourable. Nothing complicated really. And I don't play lotto.' Ian poured himself more water. 'Why are you suddenly worried about my financial position?'

'Hey.' Max raised his hands. 'Not worried about it. Just that I get a twinge of discomfort every now and then. Wondering how I'm ever going to repay you.'

'Please don't. That is, don't feel guilty and don't repay anything. I thought we had put this discussion behind us years back. Your work is the payment and that's that.'

'And what if I retire?'

'Is that likely anytime soon?'

'Don't know. Claire wants me to. And, that phone call earlier... I have a lead on Halliday.'

CHAPTER 8

THE APARTMENT

Max had just left the building which housed Hastings Psychology when phone number two vibrated. He knew it was Laura before he answered. This mobile was dedicated to calls only from, and only to her.

'Hey, Laura.'

'Max. Can we catch up. There's a couple of things I need to ask.'

'Oh, have I been naughty?' he replied flirtatiously.

'Well, that remains to be seen. Does the name John Watson ring any bells?'

'Okay, the Pelican Street apartment tonight,' said Max more directly.

'Sure. And there's Susan Mortimer's coroner's inquest too.'

'I thought that was an uncomplicated suicide.'

'Apparently not. See you at eight. Gotta fly. Later!'

The phone disconnected. His apartment was at Surry Hills and used to be Claire's main residence before everything went pear shaped. It was handy for her teaching job at the Sydney girls High School – a job from which she was now on indefinite leave.

*   *   *

The Pelican Street unit was secure. The door was double dead locked and had a strong security chain on the inside. There was also the monitor with a clear view from the front door across the foyer to the elevators. Being on the seventh floor there was little chance of anyone breaking in unnoticed, with custom locks on the external windows and sliding doors. Just to top it off, after recent events with the Mortimers, an alarm system on all entrances was installed by Max's good friend John "Dexter" Greenwood from Freedom Plus Security. Dexter lived in Melbourne, but for the price of a three-week Sydney vacation in the apartment with his wife, the deal was settled. While there was a passcode, which Max had not bothered to remember, the system used facial recognition technology and had excellent night vision. It was set up to recognise Max and Claire. In the event of any breech the system would send alerts to Max, Claire, Laura and Dexter – who, although in Melbourne, would attempt to contact Max and Claire and failing that, the local police.

Max unlocked and entered mid-afternoon. A series of rapid beeps sounded as he walked in. Then, as the beeping stopped there was an announcement in a soft and clear female voice. 'Good afternoon, Max. The security system is fully operational. My backup battery is fully charged.'

'Thank you, Tatiana.'

He unpacked a few groceries and put two bottles of wine, a shiraz and a chardonnay, in the fridge. Not that he was a drinker, but he had decided it seemed a little lame offering guests fruit juice or water. And after all, he knew Laura liked a glass of wine now and then. He dusted off a blue willow serving plate from the cupboard and set it up in the lounge with dip and crackers.

The chances of Claire turning up unexpectedly were slim. She had returned only once to collect some belongings. The apartment was another reminder of her trauma. It was in the underground carpark where she was initially abducted by colleagues of Quentin Mortimer.

*   *   *

A few minutes after eight Max was looking at Laura's green eyes and cheeky freckles on the monitor. He had done a tidy up and set the lounge coffee table with the snacks and two wine glasses. All the time he was cleaning and organising he kept asking himself *what the fuck are you doing, Max*? but nevertheless he continued.

As he watched the lovely redhead leave the elevator and walk to his door he felt his pulse quicken and felt a small anxious knot develop in his stomach. She had great taste in clothes with a preference for pant suits over dresses and tonight was no exception. The grey blazer with three-quarter ruched sleeves over a black V neck top looked lovely.

He took a deep breath then clicked open the two deadlocks and then disconnected the chain. 'Hi there.'

'Hey, Max.'

The two hugged. Max locked the door. 'Look we're matching,' he joked as he looked down at his grey polo shirt over black shorts.

'Hmm… in colours, yes,' she smiled. 'Ooh, what have we here?' Laura noticed the coffee table.

'Just a little snack while we talk. If that's okay.'

'And a little drink?'

'If that's what you want.'

'And you?'

'I'm prepared to try one glass.'

'To be sociable.'

'Of course.'

Laura sat on the sofa.

'White or red?' asked Max.

'Definitely red, as long as it's not a Rosé.'

'I have a shiraz from the Barossa.' Max brought the bottle over and poured two glasses. They chinked their glasses. 'Cheers,' they said in unison.

'The wine is a little cold, Max.'

'Sorry, should've taken it out of the fridge earlier.'

'That's a lovely plate.' She pushed a few crackers to the side. 'Is it willow?'

'I think so. It was my Grandmas. It's the only thing my sister let me have. Not that I'm bothered really.'

'It has Blue Chinese houses on it. Chinese on Willow. Very special. You've gone all out this evening, Max.'

'Really, it's the only decent serving plate in the place. No big deal.'

Laura smiled then said, 'We should probably discuss a few things before we drink too much.'

'True. So, what's going on with the Susan Mortimer inquest?' asked Max.

'Preliminary findings indicate it was most likely not a suicide. She had a scrape mark on her shin and some matching tissue was found on the ledge where she allegedly jumped.'

'Maybe she was a bad jumper.'

'Maybe… there were bruise marks on one arm consistent with being squeezed very hard. The other arm was smashed up. There were none of her fingerprints on the railing. Pretty hard to climb over a fence without touching it.'

'A bad hurdler then,' quipped Max.

'We have spoken to a lot of her friends over the past months.'

'That bitch actually had friends?'

'Quite a few. She had told some of them she thought she was being followed or stalked. The night when Claire was abducted, she had the perfect alibi at dinner with some gym buddies. They too confirmed this story. They even said she thought there was someone at the restaurant that night. A man around thirty, of islander appearance with dark, very short cut hair.'

'I would have thought she would be a dangerous person to stalk given her connections.'

'True. But it does seem she was thrown over the fence and the cliff. It was the section where the safety fence is closest to the drop off. About one metre,' said Laura. She looked at Max and tilted her head.

'Honestly, more than happy she went for the big plummet. You know I had nothing to do with that, right?'

'Yes, Max.' She touched his arm. 'I know you were not involved. If you were you would have already told me. Anyway, it's not your style. But if you had to have a guess?' She sipped her wine.

'Only one guess, and that would be her father-in-law Frank Mortimer. He might blame her for Quentin. She was a driving force behind his sadistic behaviour which ultimately got him killed. Outside of that, I got nothing.'

The couple discussed Quentin. Both knew Ezekiel was the one who ripped his throat out. Max had shared all Ezekiel's unusual exploits with Laura – at least the ones he knew about. The young man had been biting bits of people for many months. Minor injuries only for some odd religious punishment reasons that were supposed to transforms the victim's life into something better than it was. Ezekiel Kaufman was wanted by police for numerous assaults but not for the murder of Quentin which was strongly believed to be a drug related hit.

The discussion soon came around to John Watson, AKA Salvatore Lombardi.

'Watson was a guest in my bunker,' admitted Max freely. 'He paid his dues and moved on.'

'He died, yesterday.' Laura helped herself to some hommus dip.

'Unfortunate, but not surprising.' Max sipped his wine and grimaced a little at the taste. 'He was not a well man, both in body and mind.'

'As a matter of routine procedure, we had to talk to the Kearsleys.' Laura washed down the dip with some shiraz. 'They were very good. You would have been proud. Had an iron clad alibi. They had driven to Melbourne and were visiting a policeman friend, Lester King, who corroborates their story. Even had legitimate fuel stops and accommodation on the way down.'

'He's a good man, my mate Lester. Always helping people out.'

'Well done, Max. I love your thoroughness.' She leant over to kiss him on the cheek. He turned his head and their lips came together. Laura reached out with one hand and to put her glass back down on the coffee table. It fell over. Both ignored it. She grabbed his head with both her hands and pulled his face hard against hers. They toppled over on the sofa. Laura over Max. A full minute later they broke apart and looked at each.

Laura spoke first. 'Are we gonna fuck our brains out?'

'I'm thinking that is pretty likely.'

'Is that a good idea?' she breathed.

'No. It's a really bad one.' With that, Max pushed her off him then scooped her up in his arms. She continued planting kisses all over his face as he lay her on the bed.

*　　　*　　　*

At three in the morning Max carried two glasses of orange juice into the bedroom where Laura was sitting upright. She pushed a few pillows around for him and he parked next to her.

'Thank you.' She gulped it all down. 'Ah… yeah, I needed that. It's been a while for you then?'

'Too long.'

'Three times. You never cease to amaze me.'

'Sorry, but that might have to do it for the night.'

'Ooh dear,' she pouted.

'I have a little reconnaissance thing happening later today. I was

going to tell you earlier, but one thing led to the other you know...'
He kissed her. 'Which was incredible.' He ran a finger around her
lips. She let her mouth open and latched on lightly with her teeth
before licking then sucking his finger. 'Holy shit!' he withdrew the
digit from her mouth.

'I think four is not out of the question after all,' she laughed.
'Tell me, what's this *thing* you are up to later?'

Max downed his juice and took a breath. 'Charles Halliday will
be returning this evening after a short trip to Thailand.'

'Max!' she sat more upright. 'Oh, my God! I want to help!'

Max had told her pretty much everything about his son, Daniel.
The three men who were on the DVD. The two that were dead, or at
least one dead and the other now listed as a "missing person",
presumed the victim of foul play. Her efforts to get anything tangible
on Halliday's whereabouts had been no better than his own.

'I have an address at Kingsford you could check out for me.'

'Sure'

'I doubt he really lives there. But it's worth an enquiry. I want to
follow him from the airport. I may need your help with that too.'

'No problem. I'll make sure I'm off duty by then.'

'And there's one more thing you might do for me.'

'If I can,' she said with a wink.

'My good mate and counsellor, Ian Friend. Can you do some
background work. Properties he or his wife own. What he has bought
and sold in the last few years. Taxable income. This needs to be
absolutely hush hush.'

'Are you spying on your friends now?'

'Yeah, it sounds bad, I know. And I expect it will come to nothing and that would be best. I'm not sure what I'm even looking for. More of a nagging question of honesty I guess.'

'Okay. I'll see what I can do.'

Max looked to the ceiling and leant back on his arms. 'Oh shit!'

'What?'

'There's something else too.'

'Yes,'

'Ezekiel is back in town.'

CHAPTER 9

BRUCE STREET

It was four in the afternoon when Laura found an opportunity to check out the Bruce Street address at Kingsford where Halliday was supposed to reside. It was a low-set brick home probably built in the seventies. It looked a little dated, but tidy enough with some marigolds and pansies working hard to stay alive in the two gardens either side of the three steps leading to the verandah and front door.

Detective O'Donnell pushed a door bell and a chime sounded inside. The door opened to reveal a large older lady with curly grey hair, wearing an apron over a long floral dress, standing behind the screen door.

'Hello, dear. How can I help you?' She asked politely.

'Hello madam. I am Detective Laura O'Donnell from Parramatta.' She showed her ID, not that the lady paid any attention whatsoever.

'That's a lovely name. And do I see some lovely green eyes and ginger hair? And perhaps a bit of an Irish accent there too sweetie?' She spoke in a sing song manner with highs and lows as she opened the screen.

'Yes, you do indeed,' smiled the detective.

'I'm Dorothy Brandis. It's been so warm these past few days. Please come inside out of that wretched weather. I have all the fans going.'

'Thank you. Mrs Brandis.'

'Oh, Dorothy please. Or Dot if you really want to be less formal. Can I get you a cup of tea? If you want to wait twenty minutes, I'll have some hot scones for you. They're very popular you know.'

'Nice of you, Dorothy. But I won't have time for that.'

'And I suppose you've come about the neighbour's cat? Poor Pebbles. Surely it was an accident. Please follow me through. We can sit in the lounge and have a chat there.'

They dropped into two lounge chairs in a smallish room that was wallpapered with a faded floor to ceiling forest mural across one wall.

'I'm not here about Pebbles, Dorothy.'

'Oh, really. Well that's a surprise. Has my husband run another red light then?' she laughed and put a hand to her chest. 'He is so naughty and gets rather impatient in the traffic. I have told him so many times. Harry, I said, with all these gadgets nowadays you can't get away with anything. But do you think he pays any...'

'Dorothy!' interrupted Laura.

'Oh... yes dear. Sorry dear,' she stuttered.

'I'm here to ask you about a man called Charles Halliday.'

'Ah, Charlie. What a delightful man. At first, I thought his surname was *Holiday* which was very funny and a bit of a joke we shared. He is very handsome and sure to be an absolute treasure for someone,' she sang.

'Does he live here?'

'Oh, no dear. But he could if he wanted to. I'd be delighted to have him. He simply rents a room at the back. Stores some of his possessions. Not that I would know exactly what things because I'm not one to pry you know.'

'When did you last see him?'

'Oh, now…' Dorothy held her chin and thought. 'Could've been August or September. Certainly, several months back. Not exactly sure. I think he picked something up from his room. Such a nice man. Never misses a payment. It helps me out you know, the extra one-hundred and twenty dollars a week.' As the words left her mouth, she sat back startled by what she had just said and put a hand to her chest. 'Oh no! she shrieked. 'That's why you're here. I didn't tell the tax people or Centrelink.' She erupted into a flood of tears – wailing and sobbing.

It took nearly fifteen more minutes for Laura to settle her down and get more information on Halliday. He had made arrangements for Dorothy to redirect any mail to a post office box at Redfern. She had given him a set of house keys so he could drop over whenever he chose but this rarely happened as far as she knew. He was a very friendly, but also a very private man and she had allowed him to install his own lock on the store room and he was the only one with a key. It wasn't until she apologised to Detective O'Donnell for not being able to let her into the room that she asked why the police were interested in him.

'A lady has passed away. We believe she may be a relative. He is mentioned in the will as a beneficiary,' lied Laura.

'Oh, that's so very sad. If he drops around, which is probably not likely, I'll let him know you called by. Do you have a card or something to leave me?'

'I don't, but I'm sure he will know who to contact.'

'Very well, dear. The scones are ready now. You must stay and have one. I have jam and fresh cream. And I can put the kettle on. It's been so lovely to have you visit and you have been so kind,' said Dorothy now back to her sing song pattern.

'Thank you, Dorothy. That would be nice,' relented Laura. She thought of forcing entry into the room. There seemed little to gain from it, given firstly that Halliday was rarely here, and secondly if there was any evidence it would be useless in court if obtained without a search warrant.

CHAPTER 10

MR ROWBOTTOM

Thai Airlines flight THA113 was delayed two hours and not expected to land until nine o'clock. Max was aware of the delay before arriving at the terminal, nevertheless, he was still there before the original time of seven, just in case. This was his first real chance to get anywhere near Halliday.

Unless something unexpected happened, it would be unlikely he would get his hands on Halliday tonight. This was essentially an information gathering and planning mission. Care was needed, Charles Halliday was no mug.

Max was unsure how his nemesis would depart from the airport. There were so many options from limousine to bicycle. To cover a couple, he had purchased an Opal card and put thirty dollars on it. In addition, he also had a bus shuttle ticket. His Harley Davidson Road King was in the customer car park. Laura was parked illegally in a disabled car park after chatting up a security guard, flashing her green eyes and ID and giving him some bullshit police story about a wanted fugitive.

Before leaving, Max had spent a few hours at the Pelican Street apartment applying makeup, including latex and hair. Now he had successfully aged himself by at least thirty years. He had left a significant receding hairline with a few bits of wispy grey hair towards the front going back to a tidy collar length style at the back. The beard was of medium length, with some black but mostly grey, and well-manicured. The wrinkles across his forehead and either side of his nose were perfection and his best effort yet, he thought. He wore a loose fitting grey sleeveless jumper over a long sleeve white business shirt and grey trousers. Now wearing the plain glasses, he looked like an aged college professor. The fake driver's licence would be difficult for an untrained eye to spot should he need to use it. The name read, Walter Rowbottom, date of birth the first of April 1943.

Walter had purchased a novel from the airport bookshop, and, while waiting, alternated between appearing to be playing with an iPhone, with no SIM card, and appearing to be reading "The 13th Black Candle". Most of the time though he was checking out passersby, in case there was a familiar face or something out of the ordinary. There was neither.

The plane touched down at ten past nine, and twenty minutes later the first passengers, mostly those with only carry-on luggage, were exiting after their passage through customs.

There were many groups, some couples and individuals awaiting the emergence of their friends and family. Three men, two of whom looked Indian, stood holding signs with names. *Shirley & Tom Hubbard*; *Somsak "Sommie"*; and the *Gerrard Family*. Walter stood and smiled, trying to look mildly excited, as he faked waiting for someone he knew.

People paraded past him, greeted loved ones, and immediately began recounting stories about the flight and their trip. Shirley and Tom Hubbard reported to the Indian man holding their name and off they went. Then a tall clean-cut man in a blue suit marched through the exit. This was Halliday. He looked left to the waiting crowd. Walter smiled in the general direction but did not make eye contact.

On the bench seat near him another Indian man suddenly stood and held up another sign. It read *Charles Halliday.* He even shouted out the name as if he wanted the world to know. The Indian turned the sign in a semi-circle so everyone could see. Walter was slightly startled as he read and heard the name, then as he looked back Halliday was staring straight back at him and holding up a mobile phone.

Walter Rowbottom raised his hands in the air and smiled broadly as he marched straight past Halliday's shoulder to a lone lady behind him. 'Alison!' he called as he greeted the total stranger with an arm around her shoulder. Startled, she began to pull away.

'Undercover police,' he whispered into her ear. 'Go along with me. For your own safety…Please.' He moved his mouth from her ear. 'How was your flight,' he said loudly.

She looked unsurely at the college professor. 'Not too bad. A little turbulence,' she said.

'Good. Very Good. Let me help you with that bag.' Walter took her only suitcase. He took a glance around and Halliday was now with his escort, both of whom took a moment to check out the gathering before moving away.

'So sorry to upset you,' said Walter as he noticed Halliday leave the building. At the same time, a man and a younger girl arrived in front of him and "Alison". They looked puzzled.

'Jenny, who is this guy?' asked the man.

'A case of mistaken identity,' said Walter. 'My sincere apologies. I think you have a doppelganger, Alison.' With that he put down her suitcase and made a hasty exit, hurrying along the concourse trying to catch sight of Halliday. He crossed the road and then a sheltered walkway to a second road where some limos were lined up. Walter peered around a wide cement support column just in time to see Halliday close the limousine door. With his Laura mobile already in his hand he called.

'Hey,' she answered.

'He's in a black limo. Just leaving should be passing you in twenty seconds. L991106.'

'Okay, Max.'

'Please tell me you've got him?' he begged.

'Just a sec. I see one coming… yep that's him. I'm following.'

'Not too obvious.'

'Fuck, Max. I'm a detective!'

'Sorry. I'm heading to my bike. We can keep this line open. I can plug in to my helmet.'

'Perfect.'

Before he got anywhere near the Harley, Laura shouted down the phone. 'He's doubling back. Taking the off ramp to come back in along Arrivals Court.'

'What the fuck is he up to. He may have made me at the terminal. Not sure. Not that he would know my face as Walter. He did a clever little deal with the limo driver to see who was paying attention. Hope I covered it okay. He was holding a mobile up. Probably using the camera. Smart bastard.'

'We've passed the train station. Still heading back in the direction of the terminal. If he made you why is he coming back?' Before Max could reply. 'He's taking an exit. Looks like he's going to the Rydges Airport Hotel.

CHAPTER 11

RYDGES

Charles Halliday strode through the lobby of the Rydges Airport Hotel and up to one of the four white marble satellite reception desks. The entry was spacious with an expansive tiled floor and a pleasant use of shades of grey and white. Above the reception area and extending up the wall to the high ceiling was a sketch of the Sydney city skyline and Sydney Harbour in black and white. There was an information area adorned with tourism pamphlets and a passageway down which a bar and café area could be seen. Throughout the hotel there were other bars, restaurants, conference rooms, gymnasium and a pool, none of which he would be utilising on this trip.

'Yes, sir. Checking in?' asked the smiling redhead with a nametag of "Emma"

'I am, thank you kindly, Emma.' He tipped his head. 'Halliday, Charles.'

The young woman tapped away at her keyboard. 'Yes Mr Halliday. I see everything is in order. All paid for. Just the one night with us this time and an early departure.'

'Yes, very good. Has the item I requested been delivered to my room?'

She checked a little more. 'Yes, it is in your room, and ready for your use. Here is your swipe key. Room four-one-seven. Do you need assistance with any luggage?'

'No thanks. Just this one bag. No trouble at all.'

'Very good, sir. Have a pleasant stay.'

They both smiled. Charles headed off to the elevator.

*   *   *

Room 417 was quite spacious and comfortable. There were two framed photos of different aspects of the Harbour Bridge mounted over the double bed. A large TV was on the wall in front of the bed and the window to the right looked out over the terminal, where, if you were keen, you could spend hours watching planes come and go. For Charles Halliday though, this was going to be his shortest ever occupancy of any hotel room.

There was one item in the room that was not normally associated with staying in a hotel. Charles had arranged for the delivery of a brand-new racing bicycle – a *Trek Emonda SLR 8 Disc.* He could not help but to take a minute or two to admire the machine. He ran his hand across the maroon paintwork, the handlebars and seat. It was a beautiful, lightweight bike built for both speed and comfort. He had haggled the price down a few weeks ago from $11,300 to $10,120 and with a custom paint job included, albeit a temporary one. What a bargain. He slapped his hands together. 'Woo hoo!' Next to the rear wheel, on the carpet, was a small box. Inside was a battery-operated bike headlight and a rear reflector light. He attached them both. A bicycle helmet hung from the handle bars.

Now there were a few other quick chores to be done. He threw his small suitcase on the bed, opened it and upended all the contents.

There were some toiletries, the clothes he wore to Klong Prem Prison, shorts, t-shirt, a baseball cap, a pair of Shinamo cycling/jogging shoes, and an empty backpack. All his travel documents, phone and wallet were in his suit which he now carefully took off, rolled up each of the three items and pushed them into the backpack along with his formal footwear.

After changing into his cycling gear, he packed everything remaining into the backpack. He lay the suitcase on the floor and jumped on it twice, splitting the side and breaking the latches. He put on the cap then the helmet.

Charles messed up the bed, wet some of the towels which he left on the bathroom floor, left the swipe card on the bedside table then put on the backpack and left the room with his bike and the broken suitcase. He stood the broken case against a small bin near the elevator. Some hotel employee would soon enough see it and throw it out. He pushed the down button. On the first occasion when the doors parted there was a family group inside, so Charles waved them on and waited again. The second time it was empty.

With his cap tipped low to avoid being identified by any surveillance cameras he left the hotel. Halliday cycled around the back, through the international carpark and then via the exit onto Cooks River Avenue. Before the overpass he took a sharp left off the main road and met up with a cycle path, that seven hundred metres later, merged with the Bay to Bay bikeway and followed the waterways for several kilometres. Halliday sped away on his new machine.

CHAPTER 12

ENZO

Enzo Scortini wore an eyepatch over his right eye. He wasn't completely blind, but had serious right sided vision impairment, which over time he had managed to adjust to. Now he was proud to display his patch. It was a symbol of overcoming adversity. It showed what a tough street guy he was, and it was now a virtual trademark. While he went about his business of dealing drugs, he always kept a look out for the guy who nearly took his eye out – Ezekiel Kaufman.

Twenty-eight-year-old Enzo kept himself in good shape, mostly by pumping iron. He liked wearing tight t-shirts to show off his biceps, intimidate the junkies, and impress the young ladies. While he still used from time to time, he had cut his drug use back significantly since he had warnings from Frank Mortimer and threats from Frank's henchman. To make matters even better, he hadn't had any further psychotic breaks or psychiatric admissions for months – not since his encounter in Gosford with Ezekiel.

Today, as he swaggered along Goulburn Street, Liverpool, in over-sized jeans that needed pulling up and wearing his "Make America Great Again" baseball cap, he saw a familiar face. Someone he hadn't seen or supplied for ages.

Several months had passed since he had last seen Alex. It was in the same street, just a few blocks further down the road. The junkie had been in a bloody mess, sprawled out on the footpath, with his girlfriend, Gail, next to him. The blood was mainly from his own fall while trying to run away, although the burly Marco, Frank's security, had made some contribution to his injuries. That was the day when Enzo believed he had last seen Ezekiel, and the day when he hoped, with Frank's assistance, that he could get rid of him. Somehow though, Kaufman had vanished, and only the two pathetic junkies were around. Enzo had been made to look like an idiot in front of his boss, like he had spotted the wrong guy or got the wrong address. Frank was not happy. He had accused him of being doped up and resented the waste of his time.

Alex sat on the footpath, legs out straight and back against a brick fence. He leant to one side with his head against a dirty pillowcase full of clothes and other possessions. A bathroom and a laundry seemed to be somewhere he hadn't frequented in weeks.

As Enzo looked down on him, he relived the entire event in his mind. He scowled at Alex who seemed to be snoozing. 'You useless fuck!' he growled. The man didn't stir.

The more he thought back on the incident, the more he felt he had been right, Ezekiel was there somewhere, and he had not made any mistakes. Sure, he had a bit of coke on board but that only helped him think clearly anyway. He kicked Alex hard in the leg. 'Hey, fuckface!'

Alex groaned and looked up. 'Enzo the pirate. Long time no see.'

'Why are you here?'

'Just passin' through. Don't want to be a bother... any chance you can spot an old friend a taste of Tina?' smiled Alex. His teeth were discoloured and decayed. There were many street terms to describe crystal methamphetamine – Chris, Christine, Tina, Ice, Shard, Speed, Crank and many more.

'You remember last time I saw you?' barked Enzo.

'Yeah, yeah… you were not real friendly. Beat me up.'

'I didn't beat you up. You beat yourself up.'

'Whatever… you gotta top me up here man. I'll square it up in a few days.'

'You made me look stupid.'

'Come on now,' pleaded Alex. He rolled and supported himself against the wall and pulled himself awkwardly to his feet. 'I got nothin' now. Tried to top myself twice and fucked up. I know you got some. It will fix me. Come on.'

'Back then I was looking for a hairless guy. Young, fit. Speaks weird.'

'I don't know, man. Come on now. You gotta do this,' said Alex more firmly while he took a step closer to Enzo and grabbed his shirt collar with both hands. 'Help me!'

Enzo grabbed his hands and pulled them off his shirt. 'This guy,' he shouted. 'You remember him?'

'Yeah, yeah… now. Please Enzo,' begged Alex. He dropped to his knees and began frisking Enzo's jeans and trying to check his pockets.

'Get your filthy hands off me. Fuck!' He took a step back. 'I can get you some. But you gotta talk to me. If you don't, I am going to fuck you up so bad.'

'Okay Enzo. I'll tell you. Let's go. Sort me. Come on. You're the man.'

*   *   *

Enzo and Alex passed a couple of squatters as they made their way to a back room of a derelict house. The place was trashed with many walls smashed in, leaking water over rotten floor boards, tins, bottles, stinking rubbish and excrement everywhere.

He shoved the partly open door. It scrapped and squeaked across the floor as he forced it. Inside a skinny junkie girl in bra and knickers was on her knees giving a blow job to some fat dude wearing only a singlet and socks. The guy's clothes were folded neatly and sat on top of his shoes.

'Fuck off!' shouted the man.

Enzo walked straight over and punched him hard in the nose. When he fell, he kicked him in the stomach. The girl squealed and took off shouting back 'Fuck you, Enzo' as she disappeared. With his eyes ablaze and teeth clenched, Enzo leant over the man with a fist raised.

'No,' he cringed. 'I'm going. I'm going.' The fat guy rolled over, grabbed his belongings, stood and shot through, naked below the waist and blood dripping from his nose.

Enzo forced the door shut. He took off his "Make America Great Again" cap and fiddled with the inside back hem. He removed a small rolled up zip lock plastic bag. He placed his iPhone face down on the floor and carefully tipped the contents into a short line on the back. He took a biro from his jeans, pulled out the inside and handed the hollow shaft to Alex who immediately snatched it away. 'I do this. You give me info. Tell me about the bald guy. Everything,' he said firmly.

'I will. Everything. Promise.' Alex dropped to his knees and snorted the line in a second, then licked the back of the iPhone and sucked the hollow pen shaft.

'Fuck off!' Enzo grabbed his phone and wiped it on his jeans. 'Gross!'

Alex sat back against the wall next to his fat pillow case and waited. The drug dealer stood over him quietly.

Four minutes later... 'Oh yeah. Sweet, sweet Baby Jesus,' breathed Alex. 'Now we're talkin'.'

'You better be talkin', and pretty damn soon. I'm waiting. And I am not a patient guy.'

'Hey, all good. Chill.' Alex got to his feet and began doing some slow circuits of the room.

'Talkin' not walkin'. I'm listening. The hairless dude. Speak to me. Now!' demanded Enzo. With that he belted Alex hard in the chest with an open hand as he was about to do another lap. That did the trick.

'He was there that day,' said Alex. 'Before you turned up and again after you left. He was kind. Helped me up. Yeah he spoke in a strange way.'

'I fucking knew it! What did he want? Was he after me?'

'Not you...' Alex paused.

'Who then? Who was he after?'

'The *evil* one. That's what he said. Quentin Mortimer.'

'Quentin! What the fuck for?' gasped Enzo.

'Don't know. Didn't want to know.'

'Was he using?'

'No. Clean as. But he took our stash.'

'What, the five grams you ripped off Yogi?'

Alex paused and looked at Enzo. He paced up and down on the spot, wriggling his fingers and bobbing his head.

'We have a deal. You speak. I don't break your neck,' said Enzo after a moment of silence.

'You gotta promise me. I tell you everything. You don't kill me, and I walk outta here.'

'I just said that, shit head. Speak!'

'It was more than five grams. It was a K. We ripped Yogi off a full K.'

'You expect me to believe that you and Gail, two fucked up junkies, somehow managed to mastermind a plan to rip off a K of shard? Bullshit. I don't buy it.'

'We had help. It was all planned. This guy used a smoke bomb. It was easy. Even for a stupid junkie.'

'What guy? Give me his name.'

'I just know him as JC, that's all. He worked for some super rich dude who I know nothing about. No name or anything. Sometimes it's best not to know shit.'

'JC?' repeated Enzo.

'Yeah.'

'What's that stand for?'

'Don't know. But I'm certain that's what it was, because Gail shouted out *Jesus fucking Christ* when the bomb went off. It just stuck.'

Enzo took out his phone and started to make a call.

'I can go now, right? I've told you everything. You got a roadie for me? Be a friendly pirate.'

Enzo put up his hand for Alex to shut up. He moved to the corner of the room and chatted away quietly. Alex paced back and forward, wringing his hands, clenching his teeth and mumbling to himself.

'Good news,' said Enzo brightly as he tucked his phone into his baggy pants. 'You can leave here now, but you need to get outta this area. I've arranged a lift for you. I'll tag along to start with.'

'And the roadie?'

'No problemo,' smiled Enzo.

CHAPTER 13

A PRIVATE MEETING

Halliday sat in a small hotel room in Redfern. It was significantly down-market from Rydges, but it was a room, and for ninety dollars that's all he wanted for a few hours. He had paid cash.

There was a narrow desk in front of the bed. He had cleared off the phone and hotel directories and the promotional tourist booklets. Now his mobile phone and a laptop were set up in their place. Propped up alongside the bed was his new racing bike.

Since his arrival at the hotel he had showered and changed into a pair of stubbies and a sleeveless t-shirt. His cycling clothes were hanging up in the bathroom.

He checked his watch. His visitor was running late. Halliday counted out 20 fifty-dollar notes, from his wallet and placed them next to the computer and waited.

For the third time he fiddled with the air-conditioning remote which didn't want to go below twenty-three degrees and the fan seemed stuck on low. He chucked it to one side and stretched out on the double bed.

Five minutes later there was a knock on the door.

'About bloody time,' he grumbled as he jumped up. As the door opened, he saw the bearded face of his Man-Friday.

'Hey boss, sorry I'm a bit late,' said the man with a smile. 'We gotta stop meeting like this!'

'Say something original for a change, Jackson. Come in,' said Charles.

Charles Halliday and Jackson Churchill generally met in hotels and motels and Jackson's line was a well-worn one.

He was middle-aged, of solid build with moustache and beard and brushed back wavy black hair. The two men had been working together since Halliday arrived in Sydney. A police friend in Melbourne had recommended him. Jackson had multiple roles – a private detective, an IT consultant, business advisor and part time accountant. With his ex-military history from Iraq and Afghanistan he could certainly take care of himself if a tough situation called for it. As long as he was getting well paid, he was not interested in what his boss got up to in his spare time.

'Before we get started,' said Charles. 'How is the identity business going?'

Charles dragged the double bed closer to the narrow bench. Both sat down.

'Surprisingly well,' said Jackson as he dropped onto the end of the bed. 'Everything is on track. I expect I'll have a credible and legal alternative identity for you within two weeks. Passport, licence, credit card, travel documents, the works.'

'Looking forward to it. It will simplify my life significantly.' Charles handed the one thousand dollars to his companion.

'Cheers. Many thanks.' He folded and pushed the notes into his shirt pocket and did up the button.

'The current pressing issue is that I think someone is trying to follow me,' said Charles. 'I'm pretty sure I shook them off at the airport. I wanted you to have a look at these pics from my phone.'

'When was this?'

'On Thursday night around nine-thirty. Sydney International.'

The phone was connected to the laptop. Charles double clicked a file and a jpg opened. It showed a group of people at the airport, some greeting travelers and some waiting.

'This guy here.' He pointed to Walter Rowbottom. 'I had a little arrangement with my limo driver that only when he saw me emerge would he display the sign and call my name. And this guy...' he pointed to Rowbottom again, '...seemed a little surprised.'

'He looks pretty old. Seventy, seventy-five. You sure he was watching you?'

'Oh yeah,' nodded Halliday. 'He was. And he made a good cover up attempt. He called out to a lady behind me as if he knew her. *Alison*, he said. Then went over and greeted her. Arm around the shoulders and all.'

'Yeah, so...'

'Here's the thing, Jackson. That lady was sitting near me on the flight and her name is Jenny.' Halliday smiled.

'Son of a bitch!' laughed Jackson. 'Really bad luck for him. Great for you. So, who is he?'

'I haven't the slightest clue. That's where you come in. I do have some information from an old friend that this other guy, Maxwell Judd...' Halliday clicked open another picture and up popped an image of Max looking a bit younger than forty-four, '... who is a retired Victorian cop, is likely to be seeking an audience with me with a view to terminating my existence.'

Jackson showed little surprise at the statement other than a slight raise of the eyebrows. 'Could've grown the beard. But this is a different guy to the old bloke at the airport.'

'Yeah, I agree. A different guy. Although I have been told he is good at disguising himself.'

'Zoom up on the first one,' asked Jackson. Halliday magnified and centered Rowbottom's face. His colleague leaned forward. 'Still looks like a different guy. They probably work together. Looks a bit old to be running around chasing people and terminating their existence. Probably just an eyes and ears bloke. Do you have anything else on the ex-cop Judd?'

'Not much. Has kids and an ex-wife in Brisbane. May have a teacher girlfriend possibly named Clara according to my source. He's as cunning as a shithouse rat. I think he may have killed an old friend of mine.'

Charles Halliday went on to talk about Robert Mallory and what he had found out from his visit to Angel. At no stage did he give any indication as to why he or Mallory would be on an ex-cop's hit list. And while Jackson did wonder, there was no way he would ask. If the boss wanted him to know he would tell him. Termination of Charles Halliday also meant termination of Jackson's services and more importantly, a line of good income, and that just wouldn't do.

'One final picture to show you,' said Charles. He clicked open a movie file. He let it run for ten seconds then paused it. 'This is dashcam footage from the limo as we left the airport. This parked car here moved out after we went past. Looks like a female driver, right? Possibly red hair but hard to be sure.'

'Possibly,' said Jackson.

'She is parked in a disabled car space and looking my way. It may be nothing. Car looks dark coloured. I think it's a Hyundai i30. You can see the rego…' Halliday moved the video forward a few frames. 'There… 1 R 1 S S H. Irish!'

'So now we are talking three persons looking for you? And maybe the IRA!' smirked Jackson. Halliday just stared back at him. 'Sorry, boss. Couldn't resist it.'

'Yes, three. And they're the ones I know about. I want you to find out what you can and get me the info.'

'You seem to be doing a pretty good job on your own.'

'I have made a start, sure. But this is as far as I can go. You are better resourced than me. Please consider this as an absolute priority.'

'Definitely. Email those pics to me. And anything else if you think of it. I'll get back to you as soon as I can. This will consume more of my time than usual,' said Jackson partly posing a question.

'Tell me what you need. No problem.'

*   *   *

Jackson had been gone nearly an hour and Charles Halliday had unsuccessfully tried to have a short afternoon nap. It was not the business with being followed that kept him awake. Not even the potential threat to his life. It was the heightened expectation of his next visitor.

Then there was another door knock. Halliday removed a wad of cash from his wallet and stood still near the door. There was a second triple knock followed by a pause then a double knock. He put an ear closer to the door.

'Mister Jamieson.' It was an adult female voice. 'I am here with young Martin for the consultation.'

Halliday smiled. The contact information from Ross Miller was proving more rewarding than expected.

CHAPTER 14

WHAT RELATIONSHIP?

Max handed Laura his mobile phone to scan her face. She turned her head sideways, up and down a few times until the app was satisfied her image was collected by giving a big green tick across the screen. She passed the phone back to Max. He pressed a few buttons then the soothing voice of Tatiana emanated from the wall mounted speaker / scanner.

'Thank you, Max. Laura has been successfully added…'

'Wait for it,' grinned Max.

'Good morning, Laura,' said Tatiana. 'The security system is fully operational. My backup battery is fully charged.'

'That's just magic,' laughed Laura.

'When you first enter there will be a series of beeps and a red scanning light that will stop once Tatiana has identified you. If you are not identified in thirty seconds alarms will be generated and multiple people will receive messages.

'Impressive.'

And you should have these,' continued Max as he passed her a set of keys with a green tag. 'The two larger keys are for the front door deadlocks. The smaller one does the windows and the verandah sliding door. The green tag will scan in the elevator and get you to level seven.'

Laura had dropped around yesterday morning and they enjoyed

breakfast on the verandah before she went to work. They had a very open discussion about their relationship. Both agreed it should remain friendly but professional. They were, after all, working together on several matters – Susan Mortimer; John Watson; Charles Halliday and to a lesser extent on Ian Friend and Ezekiel Kaufman, who Max had not yet disclosed anything about a name change to Jeremiah Cornelius. No doubt there would be other cases over coming months. There was also Claire to consider, and Max was clear, it was his goal to have her back living with him at Oakdale, if possible. Laura had agreed that this would be the best thing for both Max, Claire and Max's children. Everyone needed time to heal and get back together.

After nodding, smiling and agreeing to all this they finished breakfast and had sex.

It was now Sunday, and after the scanning and key ritual, they were all set to go through what information they had gathered so far and formulate some sort of a plan for further investigation.

'Should I be considering this,' Laura looked at the keys. 'As any change in the nature of our relationship?'

'I think this apartment is a good place for us to work together,' said Max. 'If I'm not around you can come in and make yourself at home. Go through some of our notes. Leave messages for me if you like.'

'We have been working rather well together so far,' smiled Laura. 'So, the relationship then?' Her feelings for Max had become deeper over the past few months and she was painfully aware that the issue of Claire would sooner or later become something she would struggle to deal with. There was also a hunch that Max's commitment to having a future with his estranged partner was waning.

'We did go through that yesterday. You still good with that plan?' replied Max.

'Okay,' she replied hesitantly. Images of them both naked in the bedroom, then the shower flicked through her mind. 'I'm good with that.'

They sat next to each other at the dining table. Laura had been through her encounter with Dorothy Brandis and the secret room of Charles Halliday at yesterday's breakfast. Today she had other information to share.

'Not sure if this is what you want to hear, Max, but Ian Friend has not sold any property himself in the past seven years. His wife has sold the rural property in Melbourne where you used to work from. She made twenty thousand on the sale. No other sales at all.'

'Hmm…that sounds bad.'

'Between 2013 and now, Ian Friend, his wife and son have purchased other places besides yours. Ten houses. Three rural around Sydney.' She passed him a list. 'Four in Sydney suburbia. Two in Melbourne and one in Adelaide. And let's not forget the eight apartments, six here, including two penthouses, and two in Brisbane. Total value of all property roughly thirty-five million, give or take.'

Max shook his head. 'Shit! What does all that mean… really?'

'Most of the properties are owned outright. Only four are under mortgage. One thing for certain, he will be getting good rental income. It is not hard to buy more property when you have good equity and cash flow, but this does seem extraordinary and there has been little borrowing of money. I don't know anything about his bank accounts. It is possible to find out though. We would need to have strong suspicion of criminal activity to do this and if we push this button he will know. Not sure we have sufficient cause to go that far.'

'He hasn't been totally honest with me,' sighed Max. 'I've tried to raise this matter as best I could without causing alarm. He dismisses it saying he's done well with property. Buying *and selling*, he said. Which seems to be only half true.'

'Pardon me, Max, but is this really an issue? He has money. He shares a significant property portfolio with his family. He helps you out. Why do we need to be bothered any further? We have enough to do as it is.'

'It's not just the money, although that does get back to the issue of trust. But that whole business with Ezekiel and Quentin Mortimer. The way he put me onto Ezekiel in the first place. Sort of like he was the puppet master or something. I just can't shake it off. I hate coincidences.'

'You said he hasn't seen Ezekiel since Gosford.'

'So, he says.'

'You're not convinced.'

'No.'

'Have you asked Ezekiel?'

'Several times. The guy talks in riddles.' Max went over the events of yesterday and the conversation he had with the once-named Ezekiel…

*   *   *

…After breakfast and two serves of sex, Max had returned to Oakdale late on Saturday morning. Having done numerous double backs and fast accelerations on the Road King to be sure no one was following, he arrived home.

On entering, then disarming the house he heard a door open and close. It was Jeremiah charging out of his bedroom and going to the bathroom.

When the much-relieved young man emerged the two bald guys sauntered down the hall together. Max with his hands in the pockets of his jeans – Jeremiah stretching his arms up around his back and touching his opposite shoulder. Neither said a word.

They entered the media room. There were six recliners – two rows of three in front of a huge wall mounted screen. Each chair had a small table alongside. The other three walls were all covered in floor to ceiling black curtains. At the rear of the room, and near the entry, was a water cooler with accompanying disposable cups and a waste bin. To the side of this was some hi fi equipment and a black control panel. Max and Jeremiah sat in the front row.

'I have a simple request,' asked Jeremiah.

'I'm usually good with those,' said Max.

'When you plan to leave for an extended period, it would be of some assistance to me if you could disarm the motion sensors for the hallway, the bathroom and, if possible, the kitchen.'

'Sorry, I hadn't planned to be out overnight. Yes, I can do that. You must have been busting.'

'Let's say. My water bottle runneth over,' smiled the young man. Max sat forward with surprise.

'Wow. You said something funny. Intentionally at least. And you smiled.'

'I am but a human being, Max.'

'So, you say.'

'Ah… now you're being funny.'

'No, I am being serious.'

'Tell me Max, what is behind this curtain?' asked Jeremiah indicating the black curtain on the left.'

'A wall.'

'And what is behind the wall? I ask this because I have seen the outside and inside of this house. The internal rooms I have thus far seen do not correlate with the external dimensions.'

'What are you thinking, genius?' scoffed Max.

'I think there is a hidden room. Possibly connected with the security system, because, apart from the front door, there is nowhere else that your motion detectors and cameras could be viewed.'

'You are a clever bastard. Always thinking.'

'I do have an active mind.'

Max nodded his agreement to that but did not confirm or deny what the young man had just said. Both lay back in their chairs looking at the blank screen. After a couple of minutes Max had a question, 'Can I, once again, ask you something?'

'Please do. I will respond as best I can.'

'That remains to be seen. Mister Ian Friend, who you met at Gosford when you were an inpatient. Have you seen him again since you were discharged?'

'I believe I have answered that question before.'

'Not in any precise way.' Max leant forward and put his hands together as if praying for a straight answer.

'I have spoken unto you, rising early and speaking; but ye hearkened not unto me.'

'The Book of Jeremiah?'

'Very good, Max. With whom I have or have not associated is a matter I am not able to disclose at this time.'

'Is that what Mister Friend told you to say?' He turned to face Jeremiah who just looked back at him. The hairless young man's head tilted to one side and his eyes opened a little wider, as if to say *you already know the answer to that question.* 'Sorry, I should not have asked that. Tell me this – are you are still biting bits off people?'

'I will cure them, and will reveal unto them the abundance of peace and truth.'

'Sounds like a yes,' he nodded. Once again both sat back in their recliners and looked forward.

'Where did you go over the past few months?' asked Max.

'Melbourne.'

'Train, bus, hitch hike?'

'Ran and walked. Mostly ran.'

'Of course,' said Max as if he should have known. 'And back too

I guess.'

'Yes.'

'You left me some gifts last time you were here.'

'I did.'

'You could've driven the Monaro to Melbourne.'

'Even *you* wouldn't do that. A stolen red Monaro that belongs to a drug baron.'

'You had no choice,' agreed Max with a nod.

'You should destroy it or dump it.'

Max fired back quickly, 'Maybe I have!' He waited for a response but there was only silence as Jeremiah leant back, closed his eyes and took a deep breath through his nose.

'You smell different today, Max,' he said as he let the air back out through his mouth.

'Do I? Is this a good or bad thing?'

'To me. Neither good nor bad. To you... possibly good.'

*　　　*　　　*

'He is a strange one,' said Laura at the conclusion of Max's story. 'He seems very perceptive. Almost intuitive.'

'All of that and more,' replied Max.

'Explains why he hasn't assaulted anyone here lately. Melbourne has been copping it. I still believe he needs treatment. It's not good he keeps hurting others. Sooner or later we'll have to arrest him. You know that, right?' said Laura.

'We'll see.' This was precisely why Max did not want to disclose his name change. At least if he was going by Jeremiah, he'd have a better chance of avoiding detection. The name Ezekiel Kaufman had been on the news and in the paper, along with a poor artist's impression of his appearance. Police had interviewed many of those he had bitten, and apart from *a thinning or bald head*, there was little else of consistency among the group. No one had noticed that he had no body hair at all. There were some investigators who thought there could be up to four different people working together.

'What are you going to do about your psychologist?' asked Laura. She put a hand on his shoulder. He looked at her, raised his eyebrows and pushed his lips together. 'What is going through that handsome head of yours?' She tapped him lightly on the nose.

'I'm going to break in to his office and check the records,' smiled Max.

'Oh dear!' sighed Laura. 'There are some things you shouldn't be telling me.'

'A bit late for that I would think. And you did ask.'

'I guess so. I think I've passed the point of no return,' admitted Laura. 'What do you hope to find?'

'Something that explains what is going on. A reference to Ezekiel. Who knows?'

'Does he have alarms, security systems?'

'Yeah, but I know the codes. I even know his computer password.'

'He told you that?'

'No, no. I've been there enough times. After hours. Normal hours. I watch him punch codes in. He should change them from time to time, but he doesn't. And technically, I will not be actually breaking in. No breaking, just entering and waiting,' laughed Max.

CHAPTER 15

CHRISTMAS CHEER

Reg Christmas was the fifty-six-year-old Courtesy Officer in the Pelican Street apartment block. He lived in unit 101 with his rotund wife, Loretta. Like Max, he was a retired police officer, but unlike Max he had no level of fitness other than the strength in his beer drinking arm.

It was Tuesday afternoon when Reg finally got back in touch with Max about his request. He pushed the seventh-floor apartment door bell.

One lock clicked, then another, then the chain was disconnected. The door opened.

'Hey, Reg,' said Max.

'Hey. I see you've beefed up the security round here.'

'I think I needed to. You know I'm excessively careful.'

'And paranoid,' added the man with the round belly.

'Yes, being so keeps me in better health. Come on through. Sit in the lounge. The laptop is all set up.'

'Thanks, mate. And you should be giving me a copy of those keys. Regulations. In case of fire or something. I am supposed to be able to access all units if residents are away. All the spare key sets are securely locked up. You don't need to worry.'

'I'm sure you are very reliable, Reg. No problem. I'll get some copies made. Can I offer you a drink?' asked Max even though he already knew the answer and had a six-pack waiting. Reg went to the lounge. Max went to the fridge.

'Thanks. A beer if you have one.'

'Sure.'

'I've seen that pretty Irish lady around here a few times,' declared Reg. 'Laura the detective.'

'Oh yeah.' Max arrived with the beer. 'Here you go.'

'Cheers.'

'We're working on some cases together.'

'I guessed you were. How's Claire?'

'She's recovering. And she knows Laura and I work together. It's no secret,' said Max as sincerely as he could.

'All good with me partner. Ask no questions get told no lies eh?' said Reg with a wink.

'Fuck off, Reg,' said Max politely. 'Now, what have you got for me?' He sat down next to the Courtesy Officer in front of the coffee table and laptop.

'I have this.' He held up a micro SD card about the size of a small fingernail and no thicker. 'It's five-hundred and twelve gigabytes. Can you fucking believe that? Anyway, this is what Rydges security use. Spoke with my mate Austin, who knows Mitchel Hawkes, the security guy there. Here's the result, and it's just what you were looking for. I think that carton you promised will be in order now.'

'Let's have a look.'

'I don't think you'll need to look too far.' Reg pushed the micro

SD card into another larger carrier card which was then inserted into the side of the computer. A moment later they were looking at a long list of files, all with dates and times.

'Each clip runs ten minutes. They're all sequential. And on this card, there are three different angles for each time slot – A, B and C. A is from reception. B in the foyer. C from outside the entrance.' Reg clicked open a file named *150218A2135* and the video started. He dragged the slide control a little way along the bottom of the picture. 'Here we are. This is Halliday checking in. Only has the one small suitcase. Went to room four-one-seven. No issues here.'

Max was a little stunned watching this monster from face on, standing there, chatting up the receptionist and smiling like some sort of goody two-shoes. Knowing what he had done to Daniel and goodness what else to so many others, Max felt his mouth watering and put a hand over his stomach.

'You all good?' continued Reg.

'Oh, yes. Nauseated, but very good.'

'Okay then.' Reg took a big gulp of his beer then opened another file - *150218A2205*. 'Now check this out… here comes this dude with a shiny new racing bicycle. Backpack on. Sports shoes. Keeping his head down so cameras don't see his face, which is pointless because another clip shows him coming out of four-one-seven with the stupid bike. This is Halliday. No doubt about it.'

'All nicely planned.'

'For what it's worth his hotel registration shows the Bruce Street address.'

They looked at a couple more videos. It was clear he had left by going around the rear of the building. Apart from the broken suitcase he had left nothing else behind and never returned to the hotel.

CHAPTER 16

JC's 1st REPORT

Jackson Churchill was in his office finishing off an email. It detailed the progress of his investigations as directed by Charles Halliday. Soon he would be sending the email to one of his own Gmail accounts. An account that Halliday had access to.

Boss – here are some preliminary findings.

The bearded guy at the airport remains a mystery. I am trying to get my hands on some of the CCT footage. Give me a couple more days on that.

The car at the airport – 1 R 1 S S H – belongs to Laura O'Donnell. She is a detective at Parramatta. Age 29. Her current address is unavailable. I am still working on that too. I have attached her photo – it is about two years old. I do know that she worked on the Quentin Mortimer murder/drug case which you may remember from 5th May 2017. This is an interesting fact because QM kidnapped and brutalised Claire Kushner. Kushner is a teacher currently on extended sick leave since the incident. And this would be the person that your source told you about – the one that sounded like "Clara". I have a security friend who works for Frank Mortimer (QM's father) and he tells me that Kushner was in a relationship with Maxwell Judd!! Bingo!!

One place they used to live at was an apartment on the seventh floor in Pelican Street Surry Hills. This may still be an address used by Judd and Kushner – I will be doing some surveillance. I am also seeking alternative addresses for Kushner.

Someone is trying to find you. Maybe Judd, maybe police, maybe the airport guy or maybe other unknowns. Please remain vigilant. If you need me to step up a level and have some direct contact with any of these people, please advise.

I believe you have my bank account details

Many thanks

JC

Churchill clicked SEND.

CHAPTER 17

PROMISES & PUNISHMENT

'As shocking as this might sound. If my son and his wife were still alive, I would hand you over to them with the utmost pleasure,' said Frank. 'It is fortunate for you they're no longer with us...' Frank put out his hand and Diego slapped a Glock 19 with attached suppressor into his palm. 'So, this will be quick, and I imagine, relatively painless.' With that he put one nine-millimetre slug into the back of Alex's head. Blood spurted out of the junkie's mouth. Some specks landed on Enzo's jeans and shoes.

The gagged and kneeling drug addict fell to one side onto a large piece of old carpet. His hands were zip tied behind his back. Blood oozed through his matted hair and trickled from his mouth onto the rug.

Enzo turned away gasped, crouched and vomited.

'Diego, take a photo then roll him up. It may be useful to show his girlfriend and get her talking. Alex will need to visit Yogi,' said Frank with a grin. The short thick-set man looked around the large bare room. 'This is where my son was murdered, Diego.'

'Yes, sir.'

'The cops only released this place back to the family a month ago,' said Frank more or less to himself.

The house was a red brick, low-set home on a small disused farm at Horsley Park in western Sydney. The Mortimers had a container out the back once used for storage of drugs. Frank had been forced to make other arrangements for his stock.

He squatted down on the floor boards and pushed a finger through one of several holes in the floor. 'He made these holes so blood could drain away.' He touched a stainless-steel u bolt anchored to the floor. 'This is where he fitted wire restraints that held his victims in a torture chair.'

'Yes, sir,' replied Diego as he rolled Alex up.

'It is true. He was a monster. My own son. Can you believe that? Where the hell did he acquire those genetics, Diego?'

'Not sure, sir.' The hulk looked at the rolled-up Alex and glanced back at his boss with an unseen roll of his eyes. 'Obviously, not your side of the family,' he added.

'Quite right, Diego,' smiled Frank.

Frank was always smiling. It was more a lifetime habit than any real reflection of his mood. Speaking calmly, clearly and thoughtfully was what he was known for. The round-faced man walked over to Enzo who was still crouched down and looking away from the grizzly scene. 'I want his girlfriend. You need to find her. She is just as guilty as this deadbeat.'

Enzo straightened himself up and wiped his mouth roughly with his arm. 'Fuck, Frank!' Enzo trembled. 'I told him he could walk free if he told me everything.'

'You lied. You should not be making promises that I can't keep.'

'Look at my clothes, my shoes,' he whimpered.

Frank took out his wallet and threw over a few one hundred-dollar notes. 'Buy some more. Burn those.'

'I didn't know this was going to happen. This is not good.' He shook his head vigorously from side to side.

'Nothing happened. Best you be clear about that, young man.'

'Oh yes, sir,' he stuttered.

'Tell me,' asked Frank. 'This Kaufman character. You've met him. We know now that he ended up taking my drugs. But do you think he killed Quentin?'

'Um…' stammered Enzo trying to collect his thoughts. 'He is not a big guy. I don't think he could do it on his own, if at all.'

'Why not? He put you on your arse at the hospital. Bit your neck and nearly took your eye out.'

'Well… yes… but, he surprised me. He couldn't do that to Quentin,' replied Enzo as he moved a little closer to his boss. 'And Ronnie was outside on guard and he was flattened too. More than one person for sure, Frank.'

'Don't get too close to me. You smell bad.' Frank held up his hand.

'Sorry,' said Enzo as he stepped back. 'Kaufman is a junkie. Can't see how it would be him. A junkie would not be leaving all that crystal behind. No way.'

'He is still wanted by the cops but has disappeared off the radar.'

'Could be dead by now.'

'Hmmm… and this JC person,' continued Frank. 'He works for some big shot. Some prick who is wanting to cut in on my business.'

'I guess,' said Enzo.

Despite some encouragement from Diego, Alex had been sketchy about the appearance of JC. The guy had a black balaclava on most of the time, but he was tall and strong, Alex had revealed not long before he died.

'Your job is to find the girlfriend and keep an eye out for Kaufman.'

'Yes, sir.'

'Go to the bathroom and clean yourself up. I don't want that stink in my Lexus.'

Enzo left the room. Frank wandered around the big bare room looking up and down and shaking his head. 'Lots of stains on these floor boards, Diego.'

'Nasty,' he replied. 'Shall I put this carpet roll out back in the container?' He knelt next to the rolled-up corpse.

'Sure. We can move him late tonight. Take him on a fishing excursion.'

CHAPTER 18

HASTINGS 1066

Max took the elevator to the fourth floor at four forty-five, five minutes before closing time. Twenty minutes ago, from across the road at Hyde Park, he had watched Ian Friend leave.

As the elevator doors quietly opened, he could see Silvia standing behind the reception counter, with her back towards him. Silvia, a middle-aged busty lady, had been employed here as long as Max could remember. She coordinated all the appointments for all the partners of Hastings Psychology, ran a few errands and kept a stock of all supplies. She was encumbered with five dirty coffee mugs as Max leaned across the counter.

'Hi there, Silvia,' he smiled.

'Oh!' Her body jerked. She turned around suddenly. Some coffee dregs spilled out. 'Maxwell. It's you.'

'It is.'

'Look what you've made me do.' She put down the mugs and grabbed a handful of tissues to wipe the desk area. 'You know we're closed now? Ian's gone home.'

'Sorry, Silvia. Can I help?'

'No, no. I've got it.' She finished wiping up and pushed the tissues into an empty cup. After taking a deep breath, 'How can I help?'

'I was nearby. Just thought I could pop in and make an

appointment. Sorry to be a nuisance.'

For a moment she was quiet just looking into Max's face. 'No problem, whatsoever for you Maxwell. Let me check.' She pushed a button on the computer. 'Needs to boot up. Won't be a minute.'

'Thanks so much. How would they manage here without you?'

'Oh, they wouldn't. These people may be good at talking and giving out advice, but they have no idea how to manage their time. And they're hopeless in tidying up and washing their own dishes.'

'Clearly,' reiterated Max.

'You're looking well.'

'You're looking pretty fine yourself, Silvia.'

'Want to grab a drink after I close up here?' She pushed a lock of dark hair from her forehead and leaned a little forward. This was nothing new. Silvia had posed similar questions to Max on nearly every occasion she had seen him.

'You are persistent. Best look out because one of these days I might just take you up on that.'

'Not today then, Maxwell?' she sighed.

Max watched as she typed in the password, which he already knew anyway. B O H 1 0 6 6. Not so clever he thought.

'When do you want to see Ian?' she continued.

'Anything available later this week?'

'I have Friday at three.'

'Perfect.'

The receptionist tapped in a few details then shut the computer down once more. 'Done!'

'Thanks. I'll be on my way. Mind if I quickly use the facilities on my way out.'

'Go for it. I'll go and do the washing up. See you on Friday, Maxwell.'

'Bye gorgeous,' smiled Max as he waved. She watched until he disappeared into the men's room.

*   *   *

Max sat quietly in the toilet cubicle with his feet up. Ten minutes later he heard Silvia open the bathroom door and call his name. He kept silent and waited. After a further ten minutes he emerged. No one was around. From what he knew, he still had about thirty minutes until the security system for the building was activated and the solitary security officer did his first round. He could easily leave by the elevator and walk out the front door. Silvia would get security to deactivate access to level four so no one could come up but going down to level G would be fine.

A minute later he was booting up the reception computer. After a further two minutes he had accessed the system and opened Ian Friend's schedule. He flicked forward, saw his own name – Maxwell J – for Friday. There were plenty of other names, all with only an initial for the surname. Caroline M; Elizabeth J; Catherine L, James S and many more – nothing seemed unusual or familiar, and the more he went forward the less appointments there were to see. Now he flicked back week after week seeing who had been to see the psychologist. As expected, there were many repeat names including his own. He was sure he would see Ezekiel K. He went back a full year but there was no Ezekiel to be seen. Max scrolled back to the present day then flicked back to last week when he saw Ian on the fourteenth. When he was just about to give it away, he looked one week further back again. There was something unusual. He looked at the screen – on his birthday – Wednesday the seventh of February, were just a set of initials – JC. Not like all the others with a clear Christian name.

'Jeremiah Cornelius!' he said aloud. 'Shit!' Ian had said he was away with an urgent consult at The Sydney Clinic and couldn't see him for his birthday. 'You bullshitter!'

Max went back through the system checking for all the JCs – there were five. The first was in March 2017 which would coincide with when Ezekiel was discharged from Gosford. Another notable date was Saturday May the twenty-eighth. This was the day after Susan Mortimer jumped or was thrown to her death at The Gap. He double clicked the name JC. A *CLIENT DETAILS* window opened. But for JC there were no details apart from *JC*. He double clicked the word *FILE* and a password box displayed. Max typed in 1066 and a blank window opened. He did all this again with his own name and got the same result. 'Just as well,' he muttered.

Max decided to run a little test with the schedule. He changed the name on his own appointment for Friday from Maxwell J to Fuck U. A window popped open with the message *Do you wish to change all the Maxwell J entries to Fuck U – Y or N.* Max nodded – he was sure JC was once EK. He clicked N to leave his name unchanged then shut the computer down.

There was still at least fifteen minutes. He entered Ian's office using 1066 on the code pad. He checked everywhere, including a locked desk drawer which he opened with his penknife and was surprised to find several magazines – Horse Racing Australia, Practical Punting, Thoroughbred, Racehorse and others. This was weird. As far as he knew Ian never gambled.

Max couldn't find anything else of interest in the office. He left the premises and walked out the front door at seven minutes to six.

CHAPTER 19

CYCLING PERSONALITIES

Charles Halliday walked to his letter box wearing his cycling gear. There were three letters. Two addressed to The Householder and one with a window to Mr Michael R Plunkett.

As he ambled back to the front door, he opened them. One was a circular from the local member of parliament, another from *Yards and Lawns* offering cheap rates for garden maintenance. The third was a rates bill for $959.50. Charles looked again at the name on the notice. It was a name he would soon be seeing a lot more of – it would be his name, or at least an alternative name that he could use for travel, credit cards, phones, buying new cars or houses, setting up accounts online and with social media. He would still need to exercise some caution, but it would give him the freedom he was currently lacking.

Jackson Churchill had acquired this name from an Australian Mercenary who moved across several borders to eventually fight in the civil war in Yemen. Michael R Plunkett was killed. His body was never recovered, and no records were kept. However, Jackson had now resurrected Michael, and soon a person by this name would be flying into Australia. For Jackson this was a double win situation. He gets extremely well paid from Halliday for the new identity and he gets more still from an illegal immigrant for whom he has facilitated entry to the country. Plunkett was perfect. Both parents dead, never married and no siblings and pretty much an insular kind of character. There was some historical information that Halliday may need when being Plunkett, so Jackson had provided him with all the information he could acquire – date and place of birth; parental details, school and work history and previous addresses.

Charles placed the mail on a narrow mahogany table just inside the door. Back outside he locked the front door and opened the garage with the remote. His racing bicycle was parked next to his silver Mercedes A Class hatch and next to that was a grey 2012 Mitsubishi Lancer – Plunkett's vehicle.

Today was a rare day for Charles. A day when he would socialise with others, or at least ride with others from the Northern Sydney Cycling Club. The Tuesday evening ride started at six o'clock and would cover fifty kilometres at a fast pace. This was his first chance to show off his new machine which, since last Friday, was now lime green in colour. When at the club he ceased to be Charles Halliday and became Charlie Painter, keeping the same first name seemed easier.

He closed the garage door and took off.

CHAPTER 20

THE TEAM

On Wednesday afternoon, Max and Reg Christmas had spent an hour reviewing what they knew and were considering what options they had to track down Halliday. Reg was quite excited about now being on the team, although it was really a self-appointed role. Not that Max minded. Reg was a nice guy with some good contacts. As a bonus, his wife, Loretta, was a great cook. In front of them on the table was Grandma's willow serving plate with Anzac biscuits and chocolate brownies.

The two ex-cops had discussed what Halliday may have been doing in Thailand and both had entertained similar thoughts about the illegal behaviour he would have been engaged in. No doubt the guy was quite affluent – flying business class; hiring a limo; paying one night at Rydges for a thirty-minute stay and buying an expensive looking racing bike. The child care industry was rewarding him well.

As Reg twisted the cap of his fourth beer Laura unlocked the door and came in.

'Hi there, gentlemen,' she said brightly.

'Gentlemen! Nice. Cheers love,' said Reg with a raised stubby.

'Hey Laura,' said Max. He got up, gave her a quick hug and a peck on the cheek. Neither Max nor Laura wanted to give Reg any more ammunition than he already had. 'Would you like a drink? I have wine.'

'I could go a rum right now. What a day,' she sighed. 'Wine would be nice though. Thanks. And look, Loretta's been cooking! Thank her for me, Reg.' She helped herself to a brownie and took a small bite. 'Hmm...' she nodded her approval.

Max was at the fridge. 'Any news today that concerns the team?'

'Oh, yes.' She swallowed 'I think so.' She sat down. Max poured the shiraz and placed a glass in front of her. 'A body was discovered today. Along with a million maggots!'

'Fuck that,' yelled Reg. 'That's something I don't miss.'

'Who?' asked Max.

'Carl Mallory.'

'Shit!' said Max.

'Down in Lambton, Newcastle,' said the detective. 'Fortunately for me, I was only sent pictures and a brief report. Been dead for around two weeks. Neighbours noticed a smell three days ago and finally decided to call someone.'

'And this guy,' said Reg. 'He is related to Robert Mallory, one of the guys who kil... murde... assaul...'

'Murdered and molested my son. Yes Reg,' said Max. 'He's the brother.'

'Fuck, sorry Max.' He held open his hands and shook his head.

'It's okay. I'm dealing with it. Slowly but surely my friend.'

'It seems Robert Mallory remains a missing person,' said Laura. She winked at Max. 'And now his brother has been murdered.'

Reg knew Max was after the three men that murdered his son. He knew one was shot and killed. He did not know that Max had terminated Robert Mallory with the mulcher. And as far as he knew, Max did private security gigs for some extra money after getting a sizeable payout from the Victorian Police Department back in 2014.

'It looks like Carl was stabbed in the throat and drowned in his own blood,' continued Laura. 'We may know more after the PM.'

'What's the angle here, Max? I don't quite get it,' said Reg. 'My brain is not what it used to be.' He took a generous swig of beer.

'I was down there doing some security for a dirt track motorcycle meet last year,' lied Max. 'I made enquires at local gyms about Mallory.' This part was true. 'I think this is what caused him to do a disappearing act.' Partly true. 'Now it appears that someone else is either trying to find Robert Mallory or trying to find the person who has been looking for him.'

'And the most likely candidate is Halliday,' said Laura. 'Or someone who is working on his behalf.'

'This goes someway to explaining why he was almost expecting someone to be there at the airport.' Max picked up an Anzac biscuit and took a bite. 'These are great,' he said through a mouthful.'

'Shit Max,' blurted Reg. 'This arsehole may be after you.'

'Good. That will make him easier to find,' smiled Max. 'Mallory lived with a gym instructor called Angelique. It would be worth chatting with her.'

'The local boys are already onto that,' said Laura.

'Sure, but I'm thinking I may need to follow up on that one. *Ray* could make a return visit.'

'Ray? Ray who?' asked Reg.

'A long story. I'll take you through it later,' said Max.

The trio continued to chat in a general way about security. Reg agreed to keep a closer eye on the CCTV monitors in the complex and watch for loiterers outside. The discussion came around to Halliday and his bike. It was hard to be sure what brand of bike it was. They decided to blow up the image as best they could and start making enquires at bike shops.

'Probably a cash sale,' said Reg.

'Unlikely it will lead to anything,' added Max.

'It is an expensive machine, said Laura. 'And he would not have bought that to go joy riding. Could be in a club. We could follow that up too.'

'There are a lot of bike clubs,' said Reg. 'That would be difficult.'

'Maybe,' said Laura. 'But all we need is some video footage. At the start of regular club events. Two or three minutes. Leave that with me. I'll get a list of clubs and their regular schedules. Then we can talk about how we'll get it done.'

'We can meet again tomorrow. Same time if that suits everyone,' said Max as he looked at his companions. They both nodded.

After Reg had two more beers and eventually left, Max stood behind Laura and massaged her shoulders as she sat in the dining room chair.

'That's good,' she breathed.

'There's a lot going on,' said Max as he stared straight ahead and rolled his thumbs firmly into the base of Laura's neck. 'Do you think I'll ever get a regular job with regular pay? Being a regular person in a regular home?' I have had some comments suggesting that's what I need to do.'

'Huh, you would be bored shitless,' said Laura, then added, 'We both would.'

'Hmm… I guess we would at that.' He pushed a bit more firmly. She moaned with appreciation.

'That's the spot. Right there. And there's definitely no *regular* anything, happening anytime soon.'

'That's for sure. We need to stay on top of this. It looks like Halliday may be a step ahead of us.'

'For now, possibly.' She rolled her head around slowly with the massage. 'But not for much longer… Tell me what happened at Ian Friend's office.'

Max went over his discoveries. He mentioned the initials *JC,* saying how they were different to all the other entries, but did not say anything about Jeremiah. He mentioned the dates which were significant and the racing magazines.

'I'm seeing him again on Friday afternoon. It's not going to be a pleasant event.'

CHAPTER 21

SURVEILLANCE

Thursday morning Max was up at five o'clock, dressed in his running gear and out the door for a twelve kilometre run. Laura stayed in bed.

After six kilometres he stopped, not that he needed to rest, but he needed to think. He had come to a halt outside a blue and grey apartment building in Roscoe Street, Bondi Beach. This is where Susan and Quentin Mortimer used to live.

The more Max thought about Susan Mortimer the more he thought it was unlikely Frank was involved in her death. Not long after Quentin was killed Max had an involuntary escort, compliments of Frank's security. They took him to lunch with Frank. In a roundabout way the drug boss apologised for his family having harmed Claire. Frank told him that Susan was nothing to him anymore, that she was a deranged woman and he couldn't be sure what she would do in the future. One thing was clear. She was not involved in drug dealing and was no threat to any of Frank's business interests. Frank Mortimer went on to assure Max that he had no intentions of harming any of Max's family, he even offered him a job which was declined.

The only person with real motive to kill her was himself. She was the sister of Walter James Robinson, she was the wife of Quentin Mortimer, and she was the one who befriended Claire and planned the abduction with her perverted husband. He was glad she was dead.

*   *   *

It was ten past six when Max jogged slowly back into Pelican Street in warm down mode. As a matter of habit, he was always vigilant, looking at people, cars and bikes. He knew many regular faces and vehicles, even their number plates. Given recent events he decided to be a little more attentive today, so he slowed to walk for the last one-hundred metres to take in the surroundings. At this time of the morning, and being off the main road, there was only minimal activity. There were two parked motorcycles and a red Suziki Swift – all were regulars. The council rubbish collection truck was up the road, making a racket and slowly moving along in his direction. He looked upwards to the apartment block across the road from his own, which was not quite as high, only ten floors. Everything looked as it should be. He headed upstairs.

After some orange juice and a couple of hypericum Max moved onto the verandah and did some stretches while taking in the view and double checking the street below. A few minutes later Laura joined him. She had on one of his long-sleeved business shirts and a pair of knickers. She popped up on her toes, threw her arms around him and kissed his neck.

'Good morning, sleepy head,' said Max. He turned to face her and pulled her face onto his chest.

Across the road in another apartment slightly higher than their own, the curtains parted slightly. A telescope with an attached iPhone took a burst of images. As the two kissed it zoomed closer and took another series of shots.

CHAPTER 22

ANGEL

Max decided he should make a visit to Lambton, Newcastle and have a talk to Angelique Hawke. While it may have been better in some ways for Laura to interview her, that might raise a few departmental eyebrows as it was neither her case, nor her area. In addition, Max was considering a visit to Dorothy Brandis sometime soon and gaining access to Halliday's locked room.

*　　　*　　　*

It was a one-hundred and fifty kilometre trip to Lambton, Newcastle, so Max decided to head off early Thursday afternoon. With the possibility of Halliday looking for him, there was little time to waste. Laura would have the list and schedules for all the major cycling clubs by late morning. She would talk to Reg and hopefully they could make a start on videos of the cyclists sooner than later.

Laura and Max discussed how he should present himself to Angel. It was agreed that he needed to see her when she was alone – most likely when she was at home. Trying to see her as himself could be awkward and may set off some stranger danger alarm bells, especially since Carl was dead, the police had already been involved, and Halliday had more than likely been around for a chat. It was decided that he would once again assume the identity of "Ray" with long wavy blonde hair, a goatee and a pair of tinted squarish hipster glasses. Angel would know him as Ray from their prior meetings. It was clear she was attracted to him, but he had stood her up a couple of times so she may not be overly happy to see him.

*   *   *

With a sense of déjà vu, Max watched Angel leave the gym and head to her Toyota Starlet. She threw her gym bag into the back seat then stood there looking around before she got in the car. He had been patiently waiting across the road in his black van, wearing dark sunnies and a baseball cap. On the side of the van was a magnetic sign that read "Mac's Tree Removal and Mulching Services" along with a bogus mobile number.

Angel headed straight home.

It was a quarter past six – still another eighty-five minutes until sunset. Max parked a block away, replaced his sunnies with his hipster specs and took off his cap. Wearing his sleeveless t-shirt, Ray made his way around the corner and up the street towards number twenty-eight, wondering what sort of reception to expect.

As he stood at the front door, he noticed the new screen door, a security peep hole and a door chime. All new since his last visit. This increase in security was not a good sign. Ray flicked his locks from the side of his face, gritted his teeth and pushed the chime. The sound of a fog horn could be heard inside. He would have preferred a pleasant little jingle or standard ding dong rather than a harsh alert tone.

Watching the peep hole, he could see a hint of light coming through. Then he could feel some vibrations of very light, almost imperceptible, but quick footsteps. As he looked at the peeper it went

135

black. She was there looking out at him. He put on the best nervous look of anticipation he could manage – swallowing, biting his lip, touching his face and glancing side to side.

There was quiet. The hole was still black. He turned as if to leave, took a couple of steps and came back. He raised his hand as if to knock on the door. Then she spoke.

'You need to leave,' she yelled through the closed doors.

'Just five minutes, Angel… please.'

'I will call the police.'

'What! The police. Because I stood you up?' said Ray as innocently as he could. 'That seems a bit harsh and I don't think they would be interested.'

'What did you do with Robbie?'

'Robbie?' asked Ray.

'Mallory. Robert Mallory.'

Ray thought for a moment. His eyes flicked around then looked back at the door. 'Oh, the trainer guy. Yes…' he nodded in a faked sudden remembering of the name. 'I was looking for him to be my personal trainer, but the guy never showed up for work. I thought you two shared this place?'

'We did. He shot through.'

'I'm sorry to hear that, Angel.'

'Why are you here?'

'Can I come in. It's not good talking this loud out here.' He looked around for inquisitive neighbours.

'You need to answer me, Ray.'

Max knew she would ask this question. He had hoped he would at least be face-to-face so he could crank his charm to maximum. Anyway, here goes, he thought. Talking to a peep hole with the best bullshit story he could come up with.

'Okay Angel,' he breathed. 'This is going to sound really weird I know. But a few weeks back I had this dream about you. It was sort of good and bad, you know. You were on a cliff and frightened. I was trying to save you from falling but I could only move in slow motion and you were slipping. I was reaching out trying desperately to take your hand as you stretched back to me. Then there was some loud shout or something, like someone calling my name. I woke up in a real sweat, shaking all over...'

There was silence. Ray continued.

'Then, here's the thing... just the other day I'm in the Broadmeadow shopping centre car park and I see a green Toyota Starlet park near me. I ran over thinking it was you, but it was another blonde-haired lady. Nowhere near as pretty as you though....' He paused. There was no response. 'See, I told you it was weird. It just got me thinking a lot about you. I couldn't help it, but I had this feeling you were in some sort of trouble... I wasn't sure. Felt I needed to see you again.' Ray sighed. 'Sorry, it's stupid. I'm an idiot. Please forgive me.' He dropped his head, turned and slowly walked away.

She opened the door.

'Come in, quickly,' she said as she waved him in and looked up and down the street at the same time. Ray turned back. 'Have you seen anyone else hanging around here?' she asked.

'No. No one. What's going on?'

'Quick now, Ray.'

He hurried inside. Angel locked the door and hooked up the chain. She stood with her back to the door panting through her full botox lips. 'Oh, my God! Am I out of my mind?'

Ray parked himself on a stool, four metres away, at the breakfast bar facing her... 'You're frightened.'

'Frightened, excited, exhilarated... I don't know.' She put two fingers to her neck. 'My pulse is one-twenty. Wow! That story may be the biggest crock of shit I have ever heard in my life. Don't know. Don't care. You didn't fuck me last time you were here. This time you're not leaving until you have.' She moved slowly towards him caressing herself through her patterned ankle length Lycra. She slipped an arm out of her hot pink top.

Ray looked at her. She was a short hot package of dynamite and while Ray was feeling inclined to get wet and sweaty, Max had other ideas. He put up a big stop hand then peeled off his wig and goatee, dropping them on the floor. He took off his glasses and placed them on the bench.

Angel stopped and looked wide eyed at the hair, then back at Max. 'Clark Fucking Kent. Jesus!' she eventually shouted.

'Who are you scared of?' asked Max.

'Right now, that would be you. Also, the cops. A guy called Jones, and pretty much anyone who I think is looking weird at me.'

'I would never hurt you, Angel. But I would like to have a chat.'

'Sure you do. They all do. Fucking Jones said the same thing as he pinned me to the floor and tied me up.'

'I won't do anything like that.'

'Huh,' she smiled. 'Not unless I ask you to, right.' She was closer to him now. She moved her hand to his forehead and peeled off a strip of latex. 'You go to a lot of trouble, Ray or Clark or whoever the fuck you might be. Sure, we can talk. And you are still a fucking babe with or without hair. And I still feel very inclined to fuck you. Talk first. Fuck later. Sounds like a plan to me.' She ran her fingers over his cheek then hopped up onto a stool next to him.

Angel looked up at Max who was a full head taller than her. She told him about the visit from Mr Jones. She never saw his face but knew that he had polished black business shoes and tailored pants. His voice was deep and commanding but calm. Angel also told Max about the police interviewing her in relation to the death of Carl Mallory. She never told them about the Jones visit.

'Jones told me that you abducted and murdered Robbie,' said Angel. She looked at him. 'Did you?'

'Both Robbie and Jones are paedophiles. They are killers. They molested and murdered my son, Daniel. He was five years old. I found the DVD showing them doing so many terribly dreadful things…' Max took a breath. 'There were three of them. Now there's just one.'

CHAPTER 23

JC'S 2ND REPORT

Jackson Churchill prepared his follow up email for Charles Halliday. He had considerable success in obtaining information. He had the address for Claire, now living with her elderly parents at St Leonards. He attached a few photos of Max and Laura, both of whom appeared to be residing, for the most part, at the Pelican Street apartment and no doubt in a close relationship. He had noted that Claire Kushner owned the apartment and that there was the possibility she was unaware of Max and Laura's connection – an avenue worth exploiting if needs be.

Churchill, dressed as a business man with a briefcase, had even got right next to Laura in the elevator and pretended he was also heading to level seven, allowing her to scan her green tag, then aborting his half-hearted attempt to use the buttons himself. As he left the lift with her, he deliberately allowed his case to fall open letting the contents drop out over the floor. She had offered to help but he smiled and said he would be fine.

He listened and watched as she used two keys to unlock unit 701. He heard the rapid security beeps as she entered and noticed the glow of a red light. After pushing various documents back into his briefcase, he went back to ground level.

In addition, he had twice attempted to follow Maxwell Judd out of town but had lost him on both occasions due to deliberate acts by

Judd to avoid being followed. Judd had been riding a Harley Davidson Road King.

Churchill finally noted three other points.

Some of the CCTV footage from the International Airport carpark shows the old dude who was watching you at the terminal leaving on a Harley Davidson Road King. The same bike I tried to follow. This guy is likely to be Maxwell Judd. You were correct. He is a master at disguising himself.

As I previously mentioned, I am willing to take my services to another level if you require. Please advise. And the identity matter is progressing faster than expected and it is very likely this will be completed within the coming days.

Thank you for your recent deposit.

JC.

CHAPTER 24

UNTHERAPY

After Max kindly declined another offer of a date from Silvia, he plonked himself heavily into one of the eight soft, high-backed lounge chairs. There were four on either side of the waiting room. Only one other chair was occupied. The middle-aged lady was snoring with every second or third breath. Her mini skirt had crept slowly up her thighs and a pair of red lacy knickers were on partial view. Max looked at Silvia, rolled his eyes and gestured to the woman. The receptionist smiled, nodded and shrugged her shoulders.

Ian was habitually on time, and always within a minute or two of the scheduled appointment. Today he stuck his head out and invited Max in at three twenty-five for his three o'clock session.

'Hey Max. Apologies for the delay. Stuck on the phone trying to talk someone into staying alive. Take a seat.' Ian gestured towards the recliners not the chaise lounge. There was no handshake or pat on the back.

'Hope they were agreeable,' said Max as he sat.

'Remains to be seen. Now, what brings you here today? I thought we rescheduled a visit for April.'

'That's true. But I also rebooked with Silvia on Tuesday.'

'I realise that. Quite late in the day by the sounds.'

It had only been thirty seconds, but Max could already feel things were not going as smoothly as they usually did. Apart from an absence of any bodily contact, Ian was a little curt with his responses. His usual warmth was absent. He must know something. Probably that I've been on the prowl, thought Max.

'I was here just before five.'

'Yes, I had just left.'

'Unfortunate. Sorry I missed you.'

'So why are you here, Max?'

No time for pleasantries thought Max. I may as well just blurt it out. 'I continue to have concerns about money. Your money. Not mine.'

'I don't really want to go over this again.'

'You lied to me, Ian.'

'That would seem unlikely.'

'You said you bought and sold property. Really though, you only buy property. Apart from the Melbourne joint where I worked, you haven't sold anything for years.'

'Fuck Max! Have you been investigating me?' Ian rose to his feet and walked slowly around his office looking at the carpet. 'What the hell, mate. Why would you do that? We have a great thing going here. This is not good.'

'I needed peace of mind. I just couldn't shake the feeling that something wasn't right. I felt sick at the thought of doing it. Of checking up on you.'

'But nevertheless, you still did.'

'I might have compromised our relationship. I knew that could happen and I'm sorry for that. But now you need to be up front with me here. Be truthful.'

Ian pushed his office chair to one side and leant back on his arms against the desk. For two full minutes he stayed there taking some deep breaths, looking at Max, looking at the ceiling, opening and closing his eyes.

'I have been doing something illegal,' he finally said. 'I'm not proud of it.' His tone had softened, and he ambled back to the recliner, sat and placed his head in his hands. Max just sat listening. 'To start with it's nothing like people smuggling, drug dealing or robbing banks. Shit like that.'

'Pleased to hear that,' said Max. 'If it was either of the first two you would be spending time restrained on my bench.'

Ian raised his head and looked directly at his companion. 'You'd do that to your own friend?'

'I've had some past requests from families of victims to include drug pushers, dealers, importers, manufacturers whatever title you care to put on them, on my list. So far, I have declined, but it's a fine line.' There was a moment of quiet while the two men looked at one another, sizing each other up, searching eyes and body language for the truth.

'I've been gambling,' Ian eventually said. 'Well, not gambling as such really, because for one to gamble there has to be an element of risk. This was a sure thing. No risk. I've been working with some jockeys and trainers. We've been fixing races.'

'That's it,' blurted Max. 'You gotta be kidding me. Fixing races for all that time. Surely not.'

'See, you don't know me as well as you think.'

'So, it would appear. And this is how you've been buying more and more property?' He remembered the racing magazines in the drawer, but they were all very recent editions.

'Not anymore though.' Ian raised his hands. 'I'm out. Last time was… about nine months back.'

'What races?'

'Mostly Sydney and Melbourne metropolitan meets. Some country ones from time to time.'

'How many?'

'Hard to say.'

'Guess.'

'Over several years. Could be close to a hundred.'

Ian went through some major race events and was even able to rattle off a dozen names of horses that had won. He gave the names of jockeys and trainers. He spoke of bribes and the use of an assortment of drugs including opiates, amphetamines, steroids, bronchodilators, anti-inflammatories, diuretics and masking substances. The intention not always to make a horse win, sometimes to make it lose.

'Not proud of any of that,' concluded Ian.

'You've finished with it now.'

'Absolutely.'

'Really, Ian. This is quite astounding to me.' Max shook his head. Could it be true? A friend he'd known for so long being a virtual Jekyll and Hyde? Before now his counsellor had never expressed the slightest interest in horse racing.

'You asked me to be up front,' said Ian while holding eye contact and putting on his best counselling face. 'There you have it. I'm not hiding anything now. And you must promise me. Never speak to any of those trainers or jockeys. If word gets out, you'll find me in the gutter with my throat cut.'

Max leaned a little forward and displayed his open hands. 'I can't believe that you feel the need to even ask that of me.'

'Yes, true. Sorry. It's just such a sensitive matter. It's been difficult enough just to extract myself from the circle.'

'I guess so,' nodded Max. 'There is still something else.'

'You're the investigator. What else have you got on me?'

There was no delicate way of putting it. Max had seen his appointment diary. 'I had access to your schedule while Silvia was washing up,' he lied.

'Of course, you did. And what pray tell was so interesting for you?'

'The initials JC. These were the only full initials. At least five times. Some of the dates coincided with some past events which led me to believe that JC was really EK. Ezekiel Kauffman.' Max had not revealed anything about Ezekiel either being around or having changed his name to Jeremiah Cornelius. Maybe Ian already knew this. Maybe not.

Ian laughed. 'You are obsessed with Ezekiel. I have a patient who I *actually* call, and refer to, as JC. That's the only reason his initials are there. Everyone else I see I call them by their Christian name… like you… Max.'

Max suddenly felt a little stunned. This could possibly be true. It sounded fair dinkum. Or could it be another Jedi mind control trick? He sat back in his chair and let his arms drop over the side.

'I'm not sure what dates you are referring to,' continued the counsellor. 'But what you're suggesting, I can assure you, is a product of your very fertile and paranoid imagination.'

'You must do well with this business. There is no need to do other things. Illegal things.'

'You and I have been doing illegal for a long time, Max.'

'That's different.'

'Fixing a horse race and getting a windfall or torture with occasional killing… hmm… what is worse do you think?'

'You know what I mean,' snapped Max. 'We're helping victims and families who cannot help themselves. This is a good thing. We find justice when there is none to be found.'

'I'm not sure the courts would see it that way,' said the counsellor. Max studied his face.

'And what does that mean exactly?'

'Don't try to analyse me, Max. It's simply a statement of fact. And I think we are done for now.' Ian stood. 'If you wouldn't mind. I do have other clients.'

Max stood. 'Are we done for good?'

'I'll leave that question for you.'

'I'm hoping that sometime soon I can return here on bended knee and apologise like I have never apologised before. That would be a good outcome.'

'The April appointment will stand unless you cancel.' Ian extended his hand as they stood near the open door. After a slight delay Max took the counsellor's hand and shook it firmly. He walked slowly to the elevator looking at his shoes, not hearing Silvia asking if he still had her phone number, as he left.

*   *   *

Back in his office Ian went to the computer. Did a search on google maps for Oakdale. Zoomed in around New Jerusalem Road then sent the image to the printer.

With a red felt pen he drew a ring around a property and wrote - *Maxwell Judd lives here.* He drew in the rear access road to the property and wrote – *rear access with security detectors.* He marked an X where the shed was and wrote - *shed and secret bunker.* Finally, he put another X behind the shed and wrote – *red Monaro here.*

Ian Friend folded the map and placed it in an envelope and wrote two large letters on the front – JC. He stood looking at it, shaking his head. 'Max, Max, Max,' he sighed then made a phone call.

'Hello, JC.'

'Yes, Sir Ian. How did it all go?' replied the man.

'Could be better. Listen to me. He knows something is not right. I know he doesn't believe my story. He knows I don't believe him pretending to believe it. Neither of us said a thing but we both know he entered my office, accessed the computer, saw the racing mags. Shit, we've been friends for so long. Working together for years. I've taught him and he's taught me. He's been chipping away at this for months and I know him. He won't stop. I simply can't allow it to go any further....' Ian paused, swallowed and moved the mobile away from his mouth, then bellowed 'Fuck, fuck, fuck!'

He took a deep breath then got back to the call. 'I'll be leaving you a letter in the post office box in about thirty minutes. You need to collect it ASAP and see that it gets promptly into the hands of Frank Mortimer.'

'Yes, Sir Ian. Will do.' The call ended.

His office door opened. It was Silvia. 'Are you okay?'

'Yeah. Okay, don't worry.'

'You were swearing. Really loud. I've never heard you raise your voice in eight years. You even woke up Gemma outside.'

CHAPTER 25

PLUNKETT

'I have successfully brought Mister Michael R Plunkett back into the country,' announced Jackson proudly. 'He arrived in Sydney late last night from the UAE. We eventually solved the passport problems we were having. So now I have some items for you, boss.'

It was Saturday lunchtime and Halliday and Churchill were meeting in a cheap motel in Hornsby. Halliday, as usual, had paid cash and was expecting to stay overnight.

'You're the man,' said Charles excitedly. 'What about the guy that came over. Isn't he Plunkett too?'

'Only for the trip. And he is only staying for a matter of days. When his business is complete, he will be leaving again via an Indonesian fishing vessel. There's no worries for you.' Jackson dug around inside his brown leather man bag.

'Here we go. Driver's licence.' He passed it over. 'Visa card, Medicare card and passport. Hey, even a mobile phone registered under Plunkett.'

Charles opened the passport and saw his face alongside the name Michael Robert Plunkett. 'I'm no expert but this looks first class.'

'Yeah. That page is done with a 3D printer. Not your average 3D machine mind you. One with a price tag of over ten grand. You will need to spend some time practicing the signature. The Visa pin is four-four-eight-eight. Here is a list of his bank accounts.' Jackson handed over a sheet of A4. 'One of which you have been paying rent into. So, there's a one hundred percent return for you straight up. And you are now the proud owner of a property, Mister Plunkett.'

'Brilliant!'

'I think you can afford to pay me the balance,' smiled Churchill.

'I'll transfer the forty grand today. This is amazing,' gushed Charles as he examined everything. 'Can I be using these straight away?'

'Sure. Just get the signature down pat. And make sure you digest all the info I gave you. Some people get unstuck with two identities. You still need to be careful and thorough. Remember what hat you're wearing.'

The two companions sat across from one another at a small table near a window overlooking the swimming pool. Charles was already in his board shorts ready for a dip.

'Now the other matter,' continued Jackson. 'Do you need anything further from me?'

'I'd like to take it from here,' said Charles. 'You have been your usual marvelous self. Many thanks.'

Jackson stood. 'If anything changes. If *either of you* need any help, I'm just a call, text or email away.'

'Yes. I'll get back to you if needs be.'

'Keep an eye on the Gmail account. If I get any updates, which is possible, I'll send them through. Please take care.'

CHAPTER 26

LAMB CURRY

Max, Laura and Reg sat around a polished timber dining table in Reg and Loretta's one bedroom, Pelican Street apartment. The short and round Loretta was close by in the kitchen putting the final touches on the Indian Lamb curry.

At the end of the table was the laptop, positioned so all could see. So far, they had looked at eight videos of bicycle events at various Sydney cycling clubs. They had paused and zoomed multiple times, seen many faces, many bikes, even many officials, but thus far there was no Halliday. Reg had checked out five bicycle shops without gathering anything meaningful.

'We still have about twenty more events to cover,' sighed Laura. 'This could go on for days, even weeks and we could still come up empty handed.'

'Yes, we need a change up,' said Max. 'This is too slow. I don't think we should give up on the cycling angle, but given what we know about Halliday, a long-term strategy is not going to work. He's already out there and up to no good.' Max's phone gave a long high-pitched whistling sound.

'What on earth was that?' laughed Laura.

'I've never heard that before. Give me a sec.' He pushed a few buttons and opened a couple of apps. 'It was the security system. But everything has a green light. No breeches. Could be a power surge or something. Weird.'

'That's your secret bush joint you don't wanna tell me about,' said Reg.

'That's the one. When this is all over, I'll have you and Loretta over for dinner.'

'Make sure you get some beer.'

'Deal.'

Loretta delivered the curry in individual bowls with rice. On a side bowl she had Greek yoghurt and on another, chopped celery and tomato.

'Thanks, love,' said Reg. 'Can ya grab us a beer too, sweetheart?'

'Looks delicious, Loretta. Thank you so much,' said Max.

'Are you going to join us?' asked Laura.

'I'm not big on all this police talk. It gets me all worried,' said the round-faced cook. 'If you don't mind. I'll just sit in the bedroom with mine and watch the telly.'

'No worries, darlin',' added Reg. 'We'll be all done here soon.' She smiled, delivered Reg his beer then left.

*   *   *

At the same time as the trio were enjoying Loretta's lamb curry, Charles Halliday parked his car around the corner from one-hundred and twelve Fergie Street, St Leonards. It was a small brick and timber cottage with a front verandah. The block was narrow with no more than two metres on either side separating them from the neighbours. Interior lights and a verandah light had just been turned on.

Sitting on the verandah was an elderly couple. The man seemed to be asleep in a free-standing hammock. The woman was doing some sort of sewing and having a cup of tea. Halliday had noticed a silhouette. There was a third person inside.

Despite the sun having just set he put on sunglasses, a wide brimmed straw hat, a backpack and went for a walk.

He strolled up the opposite side of the road. When out of sight he crossed over and came back on the side of number one-hundred and twelve. He slowed as he passed and called out.

'Lovely evening for a walk.' He tipped his head. 'And for a nap by the looks,' he smiled.

'Yes indeed,' said the old lady. 'A beautiful evening. Enjoy!'

Shortly after she spoke the front door opened and out came Claire Kushner. 'Who are you talking...' her words petered out as she looked at the man walking by. He lowered his head and angled his hat to spoil her view. She watched him until he was gone.

'Do you know that man, love?' asked her mother.

'Not sure,' she said slowly. 'I have asked that you not talk to people you don't know.' She kept looking in his direction. He didn't return.

'No harm done, dear. Just a man going for a long walk. Probably been to the shops or something.'

*   *   *

'I'd like to suggest that I try to lure Halliday out,' said Max. 'I'm pretty sure he knows about the apartment here. It's not really the secret it used to be. That being so, he, or someone he is connected with, should be watching. They may have already tried to follow me, but I am virtually unfollowable if I choose to be.'

'Not a big fan of the idea,' said Laura. 'You're putting yourself in danger.'

'There is some risk, yes. I will be in a car. In the day. And I have a mobile.' Max took a big spoonful of the curry. 'This is so nice. You're a lucky man, Reg.'

'Yeah, *all my Christmas's have come at once.*' With a furrowed brow he nodded his head vigorously. '*Christmas is here every day of the year.* Yeah, yeah. I know all the damn jokes. *Christmas has come early again. His wife must be so disappointed.* They never gave me a moments peace when I was workin'.'

Max gave Laura a bemused look. She half-smiled and glanced her eyes upward.

'You'd be wanting him to follow you?' continued Reg.

'That's the idea.'

'Follow you to where? Ya gotta stop somewhere.'

'Hmm… That would be Oakdale.'

'Your secret joint. That's hours away.'

'One hour and thirty minutes depending on traffic.'

'And when you get there?'

'He's in my territory. I think I have that covered.'

'How about some company? A bit of merry Christmas, maybe?'

'Thanks for the offer. But best he just sees me in the car. And I don't think the boot is a good place for Father Christmas.'

CHAPTER 27

FEELINGS

After finishing dinner and saying goodnight to Loretta and Reg, Max and Laura went for a Saturday evening drive.

Although it was dark, Max was sure that someone had been following at a distance. This was a good sign for his upcoming plan. When they pulled up at The Gap, Max watched the rearview mirror and the car of concern glided on by and over the hill.

The couple went for a short walk to the spot where Susan Mortimer took the plunge. The pathway along the cliff and through the park was partially illuminated by floodlights, although some sections were quite dark where the lighting was too far apart.

It was nine o'clock, there were still people around – walkers, joggers and tourists mainly, but also, judging by the sounds of loud music and laughter in the distance, a few young people partying.

Max and Laura leaned over the railing. Near the horizon the red lights of a few fishing boats blinked away. Down below waves surged and retreated across the rocks. The light breeze felt cool although the temperature was hanging around twenty degrees. Laura squeezed a bit closer to Max and put an arm around his waist.

'It is a lovely spot. Quite romantic even,' she said.

'Yeah, providing you stay this side of the fence.'

'Oh, you.' She lightly slapped his arm. 'Mood spoiler.'

'A lot of people have died here over the years.' Max turned with his back to the view and checked back to where the car was parked. Laura repositioned herself in front of him looking at his face.

'Everything okay back there?'

'Seems to be.'

'Did I tell you forensics found two black wool fibres attached to Susan's fingernail?'

'Hey, no. You didn't.'

'Thought they could be from a beanie, balaclava or gloves, even a jumper. Didn't match anything she was wearing. To me, an assailant wearing a black balaclava seems more likely.'

'Still no suspects? Other than me that is,' quipped Max.

'You're not a suspect.'

'I would be if I was investigating. I'm the person with the strongest motive.'

Laura just looked at his partly lit up profile. He was a most handsome man. Such a strong jaw and lovely mouth, so thoughtful, clever, and caring... well caring to the nice people anyway. She smiled at her own thoughts.

'What?' asked Max.

'Just you.'

'What about me?'

'I'm falling in love with you, Max.'

He was momentarily dumbstruck, then tried to blurt out something. 'Well... I really care...what I mean is... I...'

She placed a finger over his lips. 'You don't need to say anything. Not now. Some other time. When you're ready.' She kissed him.

Later they returned to Pelican Street and deliberately parked in the street rather than in the underground, more secure, carpark. Minutes after they entered the building Max came back down with a suitcase which he put in the boot of the white Camry. The idea was to look like one or both may be going somewhere in the morning. The suitcase was empty.

*   *   *

At ten past six on Sunday morning Max pressed a button on his watch – fifty-five minutes and twenty-four seconds. A kilometre rate of well under four minutes per kilometre for over fifteen kilometres. Not a personal best, but still a good time. He walked up and down part of Pelican Street and across the apartment entrance a few times. He wanted to warm down but also wanted to be sure that if anyone was watching they would see him.

The street was quiet. Two hundred metres away a white van was parked. This was a new addition to the streetscape. There was no one in the front seat.

Max stopped and looked inside his parked Camry as if checking something then went upstairs.

CHAPTER 28

THE FOLLOWING

It was eight-fifteen when Max emerged from the building. Having had a hot shower with Laura, a bacon and egg sandwich for breakfast and now dressed in a smart dark grey suit and carrying a briefcase, he felt ready to take on the world, or at least Charles Halliday and any of his accomplices.

There were two items in the briefcase. A GPS tracker detector which he placed on the seat and the Beretta M9 pistol with attached suppressor. Ezekiel had left this weapon along with the red Monaro at Max's home not long after he had torn open Quentin Mortimer's throat. The weapon had belonged to Ronnie, one of Frank's bouncers. Since his police days Max had not used a gun. The last one he fired was a .40 calibre Smith & Wesson M & P semi-automatic pistol which caused the back of Leonard Campbell's head to explode, and the first of three was dead.

Choosing a Sunday was useful as traffic was light and the chance to spot a follower was much better. After thirty minutes Max had noticed what seemed to be the same white van three times. It felt a little unusual not doing his random turn offs, back tracking and accelerating to avoid detection. The tracker detector showed there were no devices attached to his car.

He called Laura and spoke hands free.

'Hey gorgeous,' she answered.

'Hey you. I have successfully attracted interest.'

'You be careful. Keep the Beretta handy.'

'Sure. My tail is a white Volkswagen van. New looking. Haven't seen the rego yet. It's been keeping well back.'

'Any chance to see the driver?'

'No. So far I can only make out one person, but then there's the back area I can't see.'

'What do you want me to do?'

'I'll make a couple of stops at servos just to see if I can get a better look. No need for you to rush. If you leave in thirty or forty minutes that should be fine. I have the GPS app open. Log in and follow me on screen. I would like to time it so you arrive a few minutes after me.'

'Okay, Max. Be careful.'

'Bye beautiful.'

CHAPTER 29

A NEW ME

Michael Plunkett had been following Maxwell Judd for nearly half an hour as he made his way along the M5, Eastern Freeway. This was his first full day as Plunkett. What a grand day it had been so far, not just using his new identity but also getting close to Judd.

It was a bit of a mystery as to where Judd was headed. At first it looked like he was doing something official or going to the airport – now though, they were heading west, and it was unclear. Nevertheless, more would be discovered about him as the day went by and this was a good thing. Plunkett wasn't confident this would be the day he could end Judd's life, and, just in case it was, he had his Pulse Stun Gun at the ready. He was so looking forward to putting twelve million volts through the man's body.

As he motored along the freeway, keeping his distance, something happened for the third time and it was becoming annoying. A white Volkswagen van cut him off. Apart from being very inconsiderate, it caused him to keep losing direct vision of the white Camry.

Plunkett's mobile chimed out with the sound of a barking dog. Then it went again and then a third time. He would have to change that annoying tone sometime. He checked the first text message. It was from Jackson Churchill and was simple enough - URGENT *read messages NOW*.

Just as Michael Plunkett was cursing about having to pull over and lose the Camry, Judd took the off ramp and stopped at a servo. Can this day get any better he thought?

He checked the next message…

If you are about to, or are already following Maxwell Judd, please stop. I have just received information from my security friend who works for Frank Mortimer. Frank and his army of goons are already tailing Judd. They are headed to Oakdale. I am informed that Judd may have something belonging to FM. If that turns out to be true, they may well do the job for you. I suggest giving this some time to unfold, it may work out in your favour. Mixing it with FM's guys would be a mistake. Go to the address much later and check things out. Good luck. I have also sent a map pic of the area with the address.

Once again, I am available if needed.

JC

Michael Plunkett sat for a few minutes. He saw Judd return to his vehicle and head off again. Still going west. He just watched. Plunkett turned the Lancer around and headed back to town.

'I think Plunkett will have to sit this one out,' he said aloud. 'Charlie Halliday has a job to do.'

CHAPTER 30

THE INVASION

As Max made his way up New Jerusalem Road, he could no longer see the white VW van. It had been there on the motorway, but after his second stop it seemed to have disappeared. Had there been a tracker on the Camry this would have been okay, as whoever they were would still know his location. How he could have lost them without even trying was puzzling. Had he been mistaken? Was it possible they were not following him at all?

He turned into his driveway. His phone beeped twice - *Vehicle – area 1.*

After reversing into the garage and deactivating the entry alarm he wanted to do two things immediately. Check on Jeremiah and get into the security room to watch the monitors.

As discussed with his visitor previously, he had turned off any monitoring of the bathroom, hallway and kitchen. Max had thrown in the rear courtyard area as well so the young man could get some fresh air. With briefcase in hand he checked the areas one by one, not finding anyone. He finished with Jeremiah's bedroom expecting him to be standing there reading the Bible. All he saw though was a neatly made bed and the Bible laying open on the pillow. There was a section from the book of Jeremiah highlighted by a red circle. He picked it up with one hand and read.

For this is the day of the Lord GOD of hosts, a day of vengeance, that he may avenge him of his adversaries: and the sword shall devour, and it shall be satiate and made drunk with their blood:

'Holy shit!' yelled Max. 'Who's going to avenge who. Jesus!' He threw the holy book back on the bed, but as he turned to leave, he noticed something separate from the Bible and bounce across the doona. It was a small flip out mobile phone. Max put down his briefcase and studied the good book. A section of the new testament had been cut out into a compartment for the device. He took the phone and briefcase with him as he made his way to the monitoring room.

In the media room he parted the heavy curtains and pushed firmly against the wall with the flat of his hand. A well-hidden, panel door clicked, opened and revealed a second steel door with a recessed handle. He entered the small room, closed the panel entry and locked the steel door.

The room was two by five metres and, as Jeremiah had cleverly noted, had been built in between the media and family rooms. Inside this narrow room was a wall with inset monitors, computers, boards of switches buttons and lights. The room was air conditioned with several comfortable chairs and plenty of water and food supplies mounted on shelves at one end above a small fridge. With everything linked in to backup battery power it was a safe, secure room with visibility to all areas of the house and property.

Max checked the computer then double checked his phone. There were no indications of any system breeches, yet Jeremiah had disappeared. Several months ago, he had done a similar Houdini act and vanished from the bunker.

After grabbing a cold orange juice from the fridge, he sat and watched the front driveway monitor. All was quiet. He sent Laura a text – *Seem to have lost my followers. Please delay arrival for now. Love M.*

Then he clicked on a camera icon on the computer screen. Two monitors immediately started a rotation through all the property video cameras. The display changed every ten seconds. Monitor one started at Area 1 – the front driveway entrance. Monitor two, at Area 6 – the garden shed set over the concrete bunker.

With nothing of interest to see, Max looked at Jeramiah's flip phone. At first, he started pressing on various icons on the screen and wondered why nothing was happening. The penny dropped and he realised he needed to use the buttons to navigate and select icons.

There were no contacts in the address book. Max selected the call log. There were only five listed calls – three incoming and two outgoing. One outgoing was to triple zero and made on the fifth of May 2017 – this was the day Claire was kidnapped and Quentin Mortimer was killed. No real surprise that the then Ezekiel would call to get help for the injured before leaving the scene. The other four calls were to or from the same number. For a second Max was stunned as he looked at the call number. Then he erupted…

'Fucking Ian. You piece of shit!'

He looked at the date and time of one outgoing call that only lasted five seconds. The twenty-seventh of May 2017 at seven-fifteen am – the day Susan Mortimer died, and the time was spot on.

Max's phone beeped twice – *Vehicle – Area 1*. He saw the white van enter the driveway. The phone went again – *Vehicle – Area 7*. Then again – *Person – Area 2*. He looked at the video from Area 8 which gave a view down the rear access driveway. Two four-wheel drives with bull bars were travelling quicker than they should along the undulating road. They didn't even slow for the gates just ploughed straight through demolishing everything as they went.

'Oh shit! This is bad. Very bad.' His phone kept beeping with alerts. Another vehicle was behind the white van. He was being invaded.

One of several phones in front of him rang. It was Dexter – AKA John Greenwood from Freedom Plus Security, calling from Melbourne.

'Hey,' answered Max.

'I have multiple alarms triggered. Are you okay? Can I help?'

'I am safe. I'll call you back. If you don't hear from me within ninety minutes call the cops. Gotta go.' Max hung up.

On the video from the front of the house – Area 4 - he saw a black Lexus pull up behind the van.

'What the hell is going on?' yelled Max. As he watched, three men in police uniforms jumped out of the van and moved to the front door. 'A police raid! Holy shit!' He immediately thought of Ian Friend and his recent words about how the courts would view his actions. 'You bastard.'

Beeps were going off everywhere. Red alert lights were flashing. Max considered his options. Security was breeched in almost every area. He leant over the desk and pulled down a large red handle.

Everything switched off. All the beeping stopped. All he could hope for was that Laura may be able to provide some level of assistance at his trial and reduce his life sentence by a few years. He left the room and headed to the main entrance.

Max unlocked the door, took a step back and flung it open. He was all ready to drop to his knees with his hands on his head until he saw the smiling face of Frank Mortimer.

'You're not a fucking cop!' he blurted.

'Very perceptive, Judd.' He walked inside. His three sidekicks followed. Max looked at them. They had on the light blue shirts, the dark blue utility vests and police looking caps but no insignias. Still, they all carried side arms, so it was a bit late to do anything but welcome them in.

'Shall I put the kettle on,' said Max.

'Walk with me, Judd. You have a nice place here,' Frank nodded with appreciation at the furnishings as they headed to the lounge. 'Lovely. Truly, lovely. And pass on the tea or coffee. But nice of you to offer.' They arrived at the lounge. 'You sit on the sofa. I'll sit over here.' Frank dropped into the recliner, pushed a button. The chair leant back as the foot rest extended. 'Oh, that's nice. Eli, make a note of this brand. I'll be wanting one of these.'

'Yes, Sir Frank,' replied the burly man with a scar on his chin.

'You were following me,' said Max.

'Not me personally. But you are partly correct. We just wanted to be sure you were headed this way. We didn't need to follow you. We had your address. Look at you, all dressed up fancy like that.

Wasn't sure you were on your way here or not.'

'You are in an exclusive club. Not many people know about this place.'

'Yes, and well done in keeping it that way. Remember when we had lunch together?'

'That was months ago. You had lunch. I just sat there.'

'Indeed,' chuckled Frank. 'Yes, yes. That was your choice. Do you recall what I said about Quentin?'

'Blood is thicker than water and you would find his killer.'

'You have a good memory. What else did I say I would find.'

'You wanted to get a red Monaro back.'

'Exactly. And so here I am. At your place. Looking for it.'

Max was doing his best to stay calm but inside his stomach was churning and his thoughts were running a million miles per hour. The three armed-men presented significant difficulty. His Beretta was in the security room – no chance of getting that. The fireplace implements may be his best hope. If he could get to Frank, he could hold him hostage. Maybe he could create some sort of distraction and somehow get to the secure room, call for help and get some real police out here.

'Why on earth would I have your car?' asked Max.

'There's the big question. If, hypothetically speaking, you did have the car then it would tell me you had a hand in my son's death. And for me I could solve two problems at once.'

'I had nothing to do with his death. Mind you, if I was there, I would have killed him. He had Claire. He was torturing her. You knew that.'

'Yes, a dreadful business. I understand the importance of family. And it must be said, my son was an animal.' Frank pressed another button and sat more upright. 'Wonderful chairs.'

A phone rang. Eli answered it. He looked at the screen. 'Hey.' He passed the facetime call to Frank. 'It's Marco.'

'What have you got for me?' He looked at the face of his employee.

'At the back of this shed. There is a car under a big tarp.' Marco held up the phone and panned around showing the area and the covered vehicle.

'Let's do the big reveal, Marco.' Frank looked at Max. 'What will we find here, Judd. He nodded to Diego. The square head pulled out his Glock and pointed it at Max.

Two of Marco's companions grabbed an end of the tarp and started dragging it clear. Frank held the phone high so everyone could see. Max closed his eyes. In that moment he thought of Laura, Claire, Daniel, his other children Jenny, Tony and Ella. Even his ex-wife, Deb popped in there too as he waited for his brains to part company with his skull.

'What is that?' said Frank with mild surprise.

'It's a.... it's an old Humber... Super Snipe,' said Marco.

'You are doing up an old classic, Judd?'

Max opened his eyes and saw the black Humber. He was confused but went straight into something he could remember... 'Still needs some body work and reupholstering but I got her purrin' like a kitten now,' he smiled.

'Nice. A great ride those old Humbers.' He looked to Eli. 'It appears your sources are incorrect.'

'I will need to have a quiet word with them, Sir Frank.'

'Hmm… you will.'

'If you don't mind me asking what sources sent you all here on a wild goose chase?' asked Max trying to keep calm and slow his racing pulse.

Eli looked at his boss.

'It's okay. You can tell him. Not that there's much to tell,' said Frank.

'We have been asking around about Quentin for months,' said Eli. 'And about the Monaro. Yesterday I found a map under my windscreen wiper. We don't know who left it. No doubt someone with a grudge against you.'

Max looked up at the big man. He had big brown eyes and a large head with a three centimetre scar on the underside of his chin.

'Perhaps a *friend* of the Mortimer family,' said Max as he maintained eye contact with Eli.

'I just said we don't know.' The big man did not flinch. 'But whoever it was, they know you and they know this place.'

'You gotta see this, Frank,' called Marco back on facetime. He held the phone up again and walked into the shed, then down the stairs into the bunker.

'Wow, Max. A guided tour of your secret den,' smiled the drug boss.

'This guy's got everything,' said Marco. 'Hand tools, electrical tools, volatile liquids...' he opened a wall-mounted cupboard. 'Drugs! Cool...' He held the phone and showed the range of ampoules, boxes of drugs, syringes and needles. He announced some of them as he looked through the cupboard, 'Midazolam, diazepam, haloperidol, chlorpromazine, potassium chloride, naloxone, adrenaline, thiopentone... even Paraldehyde. Enough junk here to sedate a herd of fucking hippos. No coke. No meth. Hey look, even intravenous fluids and shit.' He moved to the bench with all the attached restraints. 'I think your son would have loved this joint, Frank.'

'Is it possible?' cringed Frank. 'That you and Quentin may have had similar interests?'

'Not possible,' said Max firmly with a shake of his head. 'Not at all.'

'There's blood stains here,' said Marco through the phone.

'Can I show you something, Frank?' asked Max.

'Show me what?'

'I need my iPad.'

'You stay where you are. Diego can get it. Where is it?'

'My office. Down the hall second on the left. It's in the second drawer.'

Frank gave Diego the nod. Eli and the other pretend cop stood with their hands near their weapons.

A few minutes later Frank Mortimer was watching a video of Max's son, Daniel. Max lay his head back on the top of the sofa and took some deep breaths. 'Please mute the sound,' he stammered.

'Please Frank.'

Frank complied with the request. He looked at the video and then at Max. 'This is your boy?'

'That's my son. That's Daniel.'

'Fuck that!' he switched the iPad off. 'So sorry. Really.' There was a tear in Frank's eye. He blotted it with his handkerchief.

'That's why I have my area at the back. It's a special place for monsters. I have killed two of those men. Soon I will kill the other.'

'It's an elaborate set up for three men.'

'I have helped others that have had similar things happen.'

'Hmm… like community service.'

'Yeah. That's it exactly. Community service.'

'I will have that cup of tea if it's still on offer.'

'Certainly,' said Max. He stood which caused the goons to react. Frank waved at them to settle.

It was the most surreal morning tea that Max had ever had. Somehow, he had avoided execution by mysteriously having Ted's Humber appear behind his shed. Now he was sitting chatting to a drug boss surrounded by pretend cops. A guy, who without doubt, had caused many drug related deaths, destroyed families, shattered so many lives and most likely murdered who knows how many people over the years. Yet torture and molestation of children caused him some degree of pain. On one level it seemed odd, on another perhaps even drug lords had some boundaries. After thirty minutes the two men stood and shook hands.

'By chance, Max' asked Frank. 'Do you know anyone called JC?'

Max had noted the subtle change in Frank's body language, and the way he spoke, now that they were all friendly again. And the change from calling him *Judd* to now calling him *Max*. 'Is that all you have? Initials?' said Max dismissively as if he had never heard of anyone called JC.

'Not much else. Reported to be tall and strong and the owner of a black balaclava. Good at making smoke bombs. The guy has been seizing some of my product which has been impacting negatively on my business.'

There it was again, a black balaclava. Laura had made mention of one only yesterday. Although, that seemed weeks ago. And there was Jeremiah Cornelius and the JC in Ian's diary who, since seeing the flip mobile, Max was almost convinced were one and the same.

'Sorry, Frank. Can't help with that one.'

'One more for you, Max.'

'Fire away… not literally gentleman,' said Max pulling himself up and looking at the three goons. No one seemed amused.

'Ezekiel Kaufman,' said Frank. 'A young, scrawny bald guy.'

Max shook his head slowly. 'That's a name I would remember. Is he a smoke bomber too?'

'I don't think so. But I am sure he knows something about Quentin's death.'

'If I hear anything, which is probably unlikely, I'll let you know.'

'I would appreciate that.'

'Can I be quite direct with you, Frank?' asked Max.

'Please.'

'Susan Mortimer. Do you know anything about her death?'

'I know it wasn't a suicide...' he looked at Max. 'You're wondering if I had her killed, right?' smiled Frank.

Max tilted his head. 'It had crossed my mind.'

'No. I wanted nothing to do with her. Mind you, if she was standing on a cliff and I walked by, I would probably have given her a shove. But no, I didn't kill her. She said she was being stalked. Possible, given the weird depraved crap she and Quentin were involved in.'

'True enough.'

'Yes, unfortunately you have first-hand experience of that, and I am truly sorry. Anyway, thank you, Max.' The curly haired man nodded. 'I owe you an apology for this intrusion. I think whoever sent that map is trying to divert my attention. And you are the unfortunate recipient of that attention, probably due to your connection with Quentin through Claire Kushner and, I suspect, because of what you do in your shelter. You need to be careful.'

'I usually am. I need to be making some enquires of my own.'

'Very good. And I am happy to pay for any damages to your property. We have wrecked fences, gates and a good deal of your security set up. Give Diego your bank details. I will make a transfer. I'd like you to continue your good work here in your shelter if you feel able. If not, you can always work for me,' he smiled. 'I pay well.'

Max smiled back but there was no way Max would ever stoop that low. Monsters came in all varieties and Frank Mortimer was a bigger one than most.

CHAPTER 31

WHERE IS EVERYONE?

Frank and his cohorts had been gone for twenty minutes. Max had tried twice to call Laura, on the *Laura only* mobile, but received a recorded message saying *the phone you are calling is either disconnected or not in a mobile service area.* There were a few black spots on the way to Oakdale. He would try again soon. On another phone were missed calls from Claire and Dexter.

There was no doubt in Max's mind that his friend, Ian Friend, was no longer friendly. In fact, he had taken steps that could've killed him and were probably designed to do so. He had blatantly lied about Ezekiel. The reason, at this point, remained unclear but Max was finally connecting some of the dots. The race fixing story was a well-constructed crock of shit designed to placate and deflect. It had done neither. Now, an attempt on his life had failed, but there was every chance there would be another. The day had started out with Max believing Halliday was the one on his tail, now there were at least two people that wanted him dead.

There was little he could do from Oakdale now apart from make a couple of phone calls. He tried Claire, no answer, he left a short message. He tried Laura for the third time and got the same annoying recording. He rang Dexter and gave him the update on the invasion and the damage to the security system. They both agreed it was just as well it was not the police.

'Pretending to be cops is a good ploy,' said Dexter. 'Why would anyone call the police when they're already there.'

'If I had been a bit more observant, I would have known. They had nothing in their jackets. Not even the right number of pockets. There was no radio, no taser, no capsicum spray. Their guns were mounted on their belts and not with thigh holsters which would be more common these days.'

'When you're under siege decisions have to be made quickly.'

'Well, it's been an interesting day so far and it's only morning. I gotta fly Dex. Still a lot to do. Just so you know. I'll be turning the system back on for a few minutes. When you get lots of messages again, it's okay. And when the dust settles, I may need your services once more.'

'Got it. Stay safe, my friend.'

Max went to the secure room. There was some data he wanted. He pulled the big red switch to the on position. His phone let out a high-pitched whistling sound. The same sound he heard last night.

'So that's a system reboot.' He looked at the phone. 'Jeremiah! What the hell have you been up to?' Thirty seconds later the phone was beeping, red lights were flashing, and the monitors were displaying static. On the computer he searched back through video footage before he shut everything down. He soon found what he was after – the image of the fake police getting out of the van. He ran the video on super slow and was able to zoom in and get a reasonable picture of each of the three thugs. He sent each to the printer then switched the system off.

As well as the printouts, Max collected several mobile phones, including Jeremiah's and packed them in a small overnight bag along with his iPad and a change of clothes. He secured the house as best he could then left a note on the front door for Laura - *Heading to Bankstown. Go back to Pelican St. I will meet you there. MJ.*

It felt a little odd driving away from the place with no other security than locks and keys. He had a one hour drive ahead of him to Bankstown.

Max sped along New Jerusalem Road. He did some deep breathing, but it did little to settle him. He could feel there was anxiety, some confusion, and anger. He gripped the steering wheel hard and found himself sitting forward in his seat with his eyes wide open. His temples pulsated. There was more than anger. There was rage.

The Camry flew past a narrow gravel side road. As it went past a man wearing a wide brimmed straw hat, check shirt and sunnies got back into his grey Mitsubishi Lancer.

CHAPTER 32

SILVIA

Thirty minutes later Max tried Laura for the fourth time. At least there was reception and he was able to leave a short message. He tried his best relaxed voice as he spoke. *Hey beautiful. If you've been to Oakdale, you would have seen my note. If you're not there yet head back to Pelican Street. I'm heading back via Bankstown and Bruce Street. Please call when you can. I'm getting worried about you.*

He was on his way to Silvia's house at Bankstown. He had her address and phone number. She had given it to him at least half a dozen times. Regal Street was a quiet area and Silvia lived at number fourteen at the very end of the cul de sac. It was a two-story brick place with a double garage. She shared the home with her brother, his wife and their three kids.

While time was of the essence and while some inner tension was productive, he couldn't be trying to get information from people while being on the verge of exploding into a fit of rage. This feeling would only serve to cloud his judgement. Max stopped the car under the shade of a tree only two-hundred metres form Silvia's home. Five minutes of creative visualisation and slow breathing was needed. At least this was something useful he would take away from the years of seeing his therapist.

*   *   *

Silvia was in shorts and a tatty t-shirt, bent over in the front garden pulling out weeds, as he pulled up. As he opened the door, she turned to see who it was.

'Oh my God! Max,' she squawked as she looked down at herself and at her soiled gardening gloves and dirty knees. 'Half an hour earlier would have been nicer. Look at me.'

'You're looking good, Silvia. Even in gardening clothes.'

'Let me go and clean up.'

'Please. Don't do that. I just need a few minutes. It's important.'

'The least you can do is grab a coffee and sit in the kitchen for a minute.'

'Okay, but I'm in a bit of a rush.'

'Nice to have you visit,' she smiled. 'Glad you kept my address.' She threw her gloves on the ground and headed to the house.

Five minutes later they were both sitting on metal framed chairs at a round marble looking laminate table. Silvia brought over two coffees just as Max received a text on his *Laura* mobile:

Phone playing up. Have your message. Heading back to the apartment. See you there. Love Laura.

As he looked at the message, he realised there was something he had let slip in recent months. In the past whenever texting with Claire they would include the date of a birthday of someone they knew – sort of like a verification. Even when he used to chat with his old friend Lester King from Melbourne, they used to have a weather comment at the start of their conversation which indicated if all was well or otherwise. Now, Max wondered why he had let this slide. Why had he never done this with Laura. Anyway, she should be back at the apartment soon, then he would feel a tad more comfortable.

'Everything okay?' asked Silvia as she set the coffee mugs down.

'Somethings seem to be. Somethings are not. I need to show you some pictures. See if you recognise anyone that might have been to the clinic.'

'You mean you're not here to take me out to lunch?' she sulked.

'Sorry. Let's take a raincheck on that one.' He showed her the first printout.

'Have you spoken to Ian?' she looked at the image. 'Is this a policeman?'

'No. Just a poser. Do you know him?'

'No. You should be asking Ian,' she repeated.

'What about this guy?' He slid over the second picture which was Diego. He ignored her *Ian* remark.

'No. I don't know him either. He's a poser too by the looks. With a big square head.'

'Yes.' Max took it back and showed her the final one.

'Oh, yes!' she smiled immediately 'This is Eli.' She tapped on the face.

'Is he a client?'

'A regular. It would be improper for me to discuss him with you. You should know that, Max.' She looked over her nose at him.

'I know all that. Let me just say that these three arseholes and a couple of others were on the verge of killing me earlier today.'

'Oh my God, Max! Eli? A killer? He seems such a big sweetie.'

'What's his full name? I need to know. It's genuinely a matter of life and death.' Max had raised his voice and quickened his speech. He leaned across the table.

'Well okay, Max. Settle down. I hear you loud and clear.'

'Sorry,' said Max backing off. 'I've had a hell of a time with things lately.'

'I'll tell you everything,' said Silvia. 'You just need to take me to dinner sometime.' Max nodded and pushed out a smile. 'His full name is Eli Jesus Christensen,' she continued. 'We just call him JC. Quite fitting really.'

'Oh, Jesus!' exclaimed Max as he threw his head backwards.

'Yes, that's his middle name,' replied Silvia.

Max took a moment to take in the information. Perhaps the JC in Ian's diary was not Jeremiah at all. But Ian still had phone calls with him, so he is still lying about that. 'And this JC. He sees Ian?'

'He does.'

'Does he seem at all crazy to you?'

'I can't read people's minds, Max. I guess he seems as crazy as you do, whenever you come in.'

'I'll take that as being not too crazy then.'

'You are crazier now than I've ever seen you.'

'I am crazier now than I've ever felt.'

'You should book an earlier appointment.'

'I just might,' he nodded as he stood. 'Can you tell me anything else about this guy?'

'He seemed a nice guy that's all I can say. Oh yes, he had a scar under his chin. And always a lot of stubble. I can't tell you anything else without checking the file.'

Having already checked, Max knew there was nothing on file for JC. 'I need to go.' His brain was buzzing.

'You haven't finished your coffee.' She stood too.

'See you later gorgeous.' Max darted around the table gave her a kiss on the cheek and took off.

'Dinner,' she shouted out the door as he ran to the Camry. He waved back.

CHAPTER 33

JEREMIAH

Ted and Norma were having a pleasant lunch of ham and salad sandwiches and a cup of tea on their front verandah when they noticed something unusual. A young, bald man in shorts and a baggy white t-shirt running across their front lawn towards them. There was a calico bag over his shoulder.

Ted and Norma's house was a Queenslander style with four steps up to a generous verandah that wrapped around the front and both sides. Apart from a bitumen driveway and two garden beds of red roses, most of the front of the property was lawn. Behind the home was an old wooden barn, a newer green aluminium garden shed and an acre of Ted's pride and joy – his vegetables.

Ted slowly stood and dusted some bread crumbs off his hands onto his overalls. 'What the hell.'

'Do you know that young man, sweetheart?' asked Norma who hadn't moved from her wicker chair.

Jeremiah got closer. 'Hey! Can I help you?' called Ted.

The young man took a deviation to the side of the house. 'No thank you, Ted. Please continue with your lunch. I'm fine.' He slowed to a brisk walk and moved along the side of the house.

Ted ran to the side railing. 'This is private property. Stop right there!' Jeremiah slowed down a little.

'I will not be troubling you and Norma,' said Jeremiah. 'You have no need to worry. I will depart from your property in three minutes.'

'Am I supposed to know you?'

'I don't see how. We have never met.' He moved behind the home and headed to the barn.

'You must stop. I have a shotgun young man,' he shouted. 'I will call the police.'

Jeremiah lifted a piece of four by two timber that was across two metal brackets and then opened the doors of the barn. Ted ran towards Norma on his way back into the house. 'Call the police!' he instructed as he passed her. He darted into a bedroom and quickly emerged with a double-barrel shotgun. He cocked it open as he moved towards the back door and slipped in two shells.

Out the back he took a few steps towards the barn then heard a motor. He looked on completely dumbfounded as a red Monaro drove out. The car turned near him. Jeremiah wound the window down and stopped within a metre of Ted.

'Your Humber is a lovely machine and is quite safe. I will return it in due course.'

'What... why...' He lowered the weapon.

'All answers will come to you, Ted. For now, I say execute ye judgment and righteousness, and deliver the spoiled out of the hand of the oppressor: and do no wrong, do no violence to the stranger, the fatherless, nor the widow, neither shed innocent blood in this place.'

With that Jeremiah spun the tyres and took off down the

driveway leaving Ted standing in a cloud of dust – bewildered.

CHAPTER 34

CLAIRE

On his way to Bruce Street Max hoped he wouldn't see any police cars. He connected a mobile to use hands free while he kept on driving. He tried Claire once more. After a lengthy ring, which seemed about to ring out, it was answered.

'Hello,' answered an elderly woman.

'Hey, Mavis. This is Max. Is everything okay?'

'Oh dear, Max. This phone is driving me to distraction. I've tried to answer it a few times but keep pushing the wrong buttons. Not sure what I'm doing wrong.'

'Mavis is Claire there? She called me.'

'Oh, she was. She said you might call back and I should answer. So sorry for messing that up.'

'Where is she?'

'Three doors up at her friend, Sophie's place. Sophie is a naturopath and helps with relaxation.'

'Is she all right?'

'Yes, she was having a panic attack. She really needed to see Sophie.'

'Right. I see,' said Max. 'Does she get those often?'

'Oh, no. not much these days. She saw this man yesterday and this just seemed to set her off again.'

'What man? Where?'

'He was just a man walking by the house. Seemed nice enough. He said, hello. Claire just stared at him.'

'Did she recognise him?'

'Not really. Said she got this frightened feeling and felt sick.'

'What did he look like?'

'Didn't see his face so well. He had on a big wide straw hat, sunglasses, a check shirt and a backpack. I'm sure it was nothing dear, but you know how she gets.'

As Max heard these words he wondered if he had recently seen such a person. Just a glimpse. Somewhere.

'When will she be back?'

'Don't know. Shouldn't be much longer I would think.'

'Mavis. I need you to do something immediately.'

'Yes dear. Certainly.'

'You must go to Sophie's house and make sure Claire is there and that she is okay. Then you must get her to ring me straight away.'

'She will be there Max, that's where she was going when she left.'

'Mavis. Do this for me please. Do it now.'

'Okay dear. Whatever you think is best.'

'Thank you. I will be waiting for a call back.'

'Yes Max'

'Bye Mavis. Thank you.'

'Goodbye Max.'

CHAPTER 35

DOROTHY

It was one o'clock by the time Max pushed the doorbell on the Bruce Street home of Dorothy Brandis.

The older lady appeared at the screen door looking identical to how Laura had described her, right down to the apron.

'Hello, young man,' she replied in the friendliest of voices. 'How can I help you?'

It had been sometime since Max had been addressed as *young man*. He flicked out an old Victorian police ID. 'Hello, Mrs Brandis. I am detective Judd from Sydney.' Max left out the word *private,* but essentially what he was saying was true.

'Another detective…' she paused then cautiously responded. 'I am not in trouble, am I?'

'Certainly not. Just further enquires that's all,' smiled Max.

'Lucky you have your ID. Being in plain clothes, as lovely as the suit is, does make it difficult for us older folk to recognise all of you.'

'Sorry about that Mrs Brandis.'

'You should call me Dorothy. And you best come on in. I have some fresh apple crumble and homemade custard. You are most welcome to some.' She opened the screen door. 'If you would prefer a sandwich, I can prepare one for you.'

'You are most kind. I would love to try your apple crumble.' Max wanted to gain her complete cooperation which wasn't particularly difficult, but he was also starving. The early morning bacon and egg sandwich seemed so long ago.

'Oh, that's wonderful,' she sang in a high note. 'Let's go through to the kitchen. I am so lucky having all these very attractive people coming to see me. Harry, he's my husband, says that the cooking smells are like a magnet and just draw people to this house. He's a funny man at times.'

The apple crumble was in a glass dish on the kitchen bench. Every surface was occupied with some cooking utensil, bowl or ingredient. Flour seemed to be everywhere including the floor. Dorothy scooped out a generous portion then covered it in warm custard from a metal jug.

'There you are. You are going to enjoy that.' She pushed the dish towards Max, who had made himself comfortable on a bar stool. Dorothy, with the biggest of smiles, just stood and watched him.

'Would you have a spoon, Mrs Brandis?'

'Oh!' she exclaimed. 'Silly me. What was I thinking?' She found a spoon. 'Obviously not thinking at all. I do get a little flustered at times. New visitors. Good looking men.' She touched her slightly red cheeks.

'Men? You've had other men visiting?' Max took a mouthful of the crumble.

'Oh. Yes. You know. Charlie Halliday. And I told him what the pretty Detective Laura said. He was unhappy a relative had passed on, but said he would be in touch with you all about getting what he was entitled to. Yes, they were his words *entitled to*…I think he meant the money from the will.'

'This is the best apple crumble in the world,' said Max.

'Oh, you are so kind,' she said. 'Harry says I should go on Masterchef or even MKR, but I couldn't take him with me, he struggles to make toast without burning it. But I have been thinking ab…'

'Why was he here?' interrupted Max.

'Who dear?'

'Mister Halliday. Why do you think he came around?'

'To pick up some belongings. He left with a large carboard box of things.'

'Any idea what things were in that box?'

'I am not one to pry. But I did see some videos…I think you young people call them DVDs or CDs. And I saw some electrical cords. The box seemed quite heavy.

'I really would like to see inside his room,' said Max as he gulped down some more food. 'This is so nice, Dorothy. Yum.'

'Naturally, I would let you in, but Charlie is the only one with a key.'

'I understand. Unfortunately, it has come to our attention that he may have been in the possession of some stolen goods. That may have been what was in the box.'

'Oh dear. He is such a nice man. Very attractive too. He wouldn't steal. I can't believe that. Not Charlie.'

'Nothing too serious, Dorothy. You are quite right. He didn't steal anything himself. He would have mistakenly purchased them from someone else. But I do need to check the room.'

'Oh, I knew he wouldn't steal. But I'm sorry, I have no way of letting you in.'

'If you would allow me...' Max ate more crumble. 'Oh, so tasty and crumbly... I can break in. The department will fully pay for any damage to the lock or door.'

A minute later Max stood at the bedroom door. It was deadlocked. It took four hefty lunges with his shoulder before the wood door frame splintered and the door flew open.

'Oh, my goodness,' squealed Dorothy.

The room was just that. A polished bare wood floor. A built-in wardrobe. No furniture. Max checked the built-in cupboard and drawers. There was nothing there, but there was one item taped to the window. An envelope. Max walked over. As he got closer, he read the writing on the front. *To Maxwell Judd.*

He opened it and read the brief typed note inside:

I have lost some friends.

Balance is to be restored.

And Ross Miller sends his regards.

Max pushed the note into the inside pocket of his suit coat. He turned and stood in front of Dorothy.

'Apologies for the damage.' Max took out his wallet and gave her three hundred dollars. 'That should cover it. Many thanks. Goodbye Mrs Brandis.' He turned and jogged to the car.

'Call me Dorothy. And you haven't finished your crumble.'

Once again someone was talking to his back as he departed.

The tyres of the Camry squealed as he took off.

He still had not received a call back about Claire. How long does it take someone to walk three doors down the street, give a message and make a phone call? Things seemed to be conspiring against him. The momentary tension release he bought with his five minutes of relaxation had long run out.

He made a conscious decision to disregard all the speed signs and planted his foot on the accelerator.

CHAPTER 36

AN UNWELCOME VISITOR

Reg Christmas had spent more time than usual in the apartment foyer and in the street just outside the main entrance keeping an eye out for anything unusual, or the face of Charles Halliday.

As he stood outside looking up Pelican Street and quietly cursing some young people on electric scooters, the shape of someone walking behind him and into the building caught his eye. He turned to see a man wearing a wide brimmed straw hat, dark sunnies, check shirt and backpack march straight on through, past the post boxes and reception, through the sliding doors and to the elevator.

He was unfamiliar. Reg followed him inside and stood next to him at the lifts. The man had his head angled down and hands pushed into his jeans. The doors slid open and they both got in.

With a gloved hand the man scanned a green tag and pushed number seven. At the same time Reg went to push a button but stopped as number seven lit up. 'Ah same level,' he said. He was surprised to notice the latex glove. The man gave the slightest head nod but said nothing. Reg was still unable to get a good look at his face. The lift doors opened. The man went to the right, Reg feigned moving to the left. The only unit to the right was 701 and this guy was not Max.

'Excuse me, sir,' said Reg firmly. 'I am the Courtesy Officer here. Can I help you?' The man stopped and took three steps backwards, spun around sharply and threw a hand into Reg's face slamming the back of his head into the side of the open lift door. Reg dropped like a stone, unconscious. A small trickle of blood ran onto the carpet of the elevator. The doors went to close, but Reg was part in and part out, so they opened again. The man moved to unit 701. With the keys attached to the green tag he unlocked both deadlocks and opened the door and went inside.

He placed the backpack on the dining table. A red light was flashing across his face. Charles Halliday unzipped the bag and put his hand inside a plastic bag inside the backpack. He grabbed something firmly and lifted it upwards.

'Good afternoon, Laura,' said Tatiana brightly. 'The security system is fully operational. My backup battery is fully charged.'

Halliday had a handful of red hair. He placed Laura's severed head on Grandma's blue willow plate. Her eyes were wide open.

*　　　*　　　*

Max was ten minutes away from the apartment when his mobile beeped. He checked the display and tapped to open the notification. There was a big green tick and the words *Laura has entered*.

'Oh, thank God,' he sighed with relief. He slowed his driving.

*　　　*　　　*

Halliday dipped back into the backpack and removed two severed hands and placed them on the plate alongside Laura's head. He wasn't sure whether fingerprints would also be required so he wasn't taking any chances. His job was done, now it was time to leave.

Back at the elevator the door was still opening and closing on Reg. Halliday pulled him out by the feet and pressed G.

*   *   *

Five minutes later Reg stirred and propped himself up against the wall and felt the back of his head. He had blood on his hand.

'Son of a bitch!' He dragged himself to his feet and pulled out his mobile. The door of unit 701 was open. He staggered over still unsure if anyone was inside. 'Hey!' he shouted. 'I've called the police. They'll be here in a few minutes.'

This was not quite true, but he had punched in triple zero and had the green call button under his thumb. Step by step he entered the apartment. 'I'm coming in!' He noticed the set of keys on the floor.

He moved through the entry way and turned to face the dining room. 'Oh, my Lord Jesus!' Reg reversed out with a hand over his mouth gagging. He pushed the call button and went back to the wall and let himself slide down until he was sitting on the floor. He spoke to the operator.

*   *   *

As Reg sat panting against the wall, waiting for the police, the elevator doors opened and out walked Max carrying his overnight bag. Reg tried to get to his feet without success and just dropped back down. There was a smear of blood down the wall from the back of his head.

'Bloody hell, Reg,' said Max squatting down in front of him. 'Are you all right? What happened?'

195

Reg just stared at him and trembled. Max pushed his overnight bag to one side and took Reg by the shoulders, scanning his wet eyes. 'What?' He saw the open door. 'Laura!'

'Don't go in,' shouted Reg. 'Max! Max!' There was no stopping him. Reg cried and tried to stand again, adding another smudge to the last. Not a sound came from the apartment. The courtesy officer eventually managed to get vertical and staggered through the open apartment door.

CHAPTER 37

DEVASTATION

The police were checking the street and other apartments for the offender or any relevant information. The surly Senior Sergeant David Heath was coordinating activities. Laura O'Donnell had been his protégé, and while he was immensely distressed, he was going about his job methodically and meticulously. That was the least he could do. Forensic officers, dressed in white coveralls, were on site taking multiple swabs from all the rooms, dusting for fingerprints and photographing everything.

Max was under police guard in unit 702 which had been seconded for temporary use. The only words he could manage were *Claire Kushner. In danger. Guard her* and then her phone number. Heath made the call. The detective spoke to Mavis, her mother, got assurances Claire was safe and sent a squad car to the Fergie Street address.

Reg had been patched up by ambulance officers and then interviewed. He provided some limited information to David Heath but needed to talk to Max before disclosing the name Charles Halliday. Given what had happened, he couldn't help thinking that Max should've given the DVD to police instead of taking matters into his own hands. Reg had been adamant that Max was not in any way responsible, but Heath was not buying it and said that Judd may well be an accomplice.

The Senior Sergeant knew about Judd from contact some months ago with Judd's old boss, Senior Sergeant Scott Freeman from Melbourne. The vigilante behaviour of Maxwell Judd had been discussed. This, thought Heath, is what has got Laura killed. While he may not have killed her with his own hand, he has set all of this in motion and now she is dead.

Heath entered the lounge room of Unit 702. Max sat motionless on the sofa staring straight ahead at a small shelf supporting three ceramic porcelain models of contented looking cats. The detective carried over a dining chair, put it down with the back facing Max, straddled it and looked at the stunned man. Another police officer stood nearby.

'We need to talk, Judd,' he said as he leaned forward over the back of the chair. 'What were you working on? Who were you investigating? Why would Claire be in danger?'

Max's face was slightly pale with a light sweat. He blinked a few times.

Heath waited a moment. There was no response. 'You should know that Claire is safe. I'm leaving a squad car and two officers there until we get on top of this.' He paused again but Max still appeared detached. 'I know what you get up to... helping victims... catching offenders. It's admirable, but as you well know, unlawful. We found all your makeup, the wigs, the latex. You are a clever bastard, Judd. Do you have another base you work from?'

Max wondered if the cats were modelled on real cats or simply done from photographs.

'Laura and you,' continued the senior sergeant. 'An item, yes? Some of her hair was found in your bedroom. You have manipulated her for your own ends, Judd. Why do you have lists of cycling clubs? Come on, no more secrets. It's far too late for that.'

Max made the slightest of grunts. Are they mass produced? Perhaps they're made in China.

'I'm sure you know that she wasn't killed in the apartment. I need your help here, Judd. I need to find the rest of her body. Give me something. You have to accept some level of responsibility for this.'

Max took in two deep breaths. The smaller one has a softer face. Probably much younger than the other two. There was a grinding sound.

'You have a poor partner history, Judd. Divorced from your wife. Claire Kushner shot in Brisbane. Then she was kidnapped and stabbed by Mortimer,' said Heath loudly. 'Now a friend of mine and a lover of yours has been beheaded. Fuck me!' The grinding was louder. It was Max's teeth.

Max sprang to his feet and with his face contorted in rage screamed and kept screaming. Dribble flowed from his mouth. He sucked in a breath and screamed again and again. The other police officer held out his taser. Heath held up his hand to prevent him firing. Through the screams, tears cascaded down Max's face. Other police appeared at the doorway. David Heath remained seated. When the screaming eventually settled, he stood up and positioned himself in front of Max.

'Who did this, Judd?' he said softly.

'I will find him,' breathed Max.

'Find who?'

'I will find him, Daniel,' cried Max.

After a further thirty minutes Heath had not gained anything of any use from Max. Charging him with anything at this time of overwhelming grief would not help anyone. Not that there was anything to charge him with, although Heath was sure he could whip up something if necessary. Arrangements were made for him to stay with Reg Christmas. Unit 701 would be out of bounds for some time. Heath told Reg he would be back tomorrow after Max had a night to rest. He cautioned Reg about withholding evidence.

CHAPTER 38

THE EVENING NEWS

It was seven o'clock when Loretta served the lasagne. She did her best but could not persuade Max to drag himself from the sofa where he lay. He had finally got out of his suit, which forensics wanted anyway, and was permitted to grab some shorts and a button up shirt from the apartment after they were checked by police.

Loretta put a plate near him on the coffee table.

Reg picked away at his bowl of food for a few minutes then got up and poured himself another double scotch. No one was saying much. Before he sat down, he walked over to Max as he pulled a few items from his pockets. He placed a handful of fake ID's on the coffee table. The top one showed the bearded face and details of Walter Rowbottom.

'I grabbed this stuff and your overnight bag before the cops arrived. Seemed like a good idea at the time,' said Reg. He parked himself on the sofa pushed against Max's outstretched legs. 'Heath will be on your case again tomorrow. You'll need some plausible story for him. And he's impounded your Camry pending forensic analysis.'

Max was studying the white ceiling and discovered there were three subtle shades of white.

'No clear ID of the guy,' continued Reg. 'But we both know it was Halliday. He was wearing latex gloves. Forensics will find nothing. We gotta find Laura's body, Max. We just gotta.' He took a generous gulp of the scotch. 'This is so fucked up.'

There was a small black dot. Max wasn't sure if it was a bug or not. Could be some imperfection in the paintwork. Maybe a splatter from something.

A slightly muffled, old style ring tone emanated from the overnight bag alongside the coffee table. Max turned his head a little.

'Oh shit!' exclaimed Reg. 'Who the fuck would that be?' Max made no effort to get it, so Reg rummaged through the bag, discarding several mobiles until he found the ringing flip phone. 'Yeah. Who's this?' he answered.

'Hello, I would like to speak with Max if you would be so kind.'

'Hey, big guy,' he tapped Max on the leg. 'Some joker wants to speak to you.' Max went back to studying the ceiling.

'Sorry, but he is unable to speak to you just now,' said Reg. 'Who am I speaking to?'

'Please sir. I am a friend. I know he is in your care. Thank you for that. Can you simply put the phone to his ear, and I will address him?'

'He's not really well-grounded right now.'

'I know. But he will hear me. Please sir.'

'Okay… hey Max I'm just putting the phone to your ear. This guy says he's a friend and wants to talk to you.' Reg held the phone. 'Okay go ahead, talk,' he called out.

'Hello Max. This is Jeremiah. I know a great loss has befallen you. A tragedy of such great proportions and for that I am so deeply and genuinely sorry. I was not there to save Laura. Why the Lord did not direct me I cannot say. But I have located the evil doer. He is but metres away from me as we speak. And I have Laura's body...'

Max slowly sat up and took hold of the phone himself. Reg stood.

Jeremiah continued. 'And death shall be chosen rather than life by all the residue of them that remain of this evil family, which remain in all the places whither I have driven them...'

Max took a mouthful of lasagne.

'...Have tonight for yourself. Go through your despair. Tomorrow seek an enabling emotion. We need to act. We have work to do. I will await your presence near Sydney Park on Euston Road at seven-thirty in the morning. I will be parked there in a red Monaro.' The call disconnected.

'I'll need your car keys,' said Max. 'I leave early in the morning.'

Reg handed them over without a second thought. 'Shall I tag al...'

'No,' interrupted Max. He resumed a horizontal position and focused on the white.

CHAPTER 39

SYDNEY PARK

Max was on autopilot for the forty-minute drive to Sydney Park. As he read the Euston Road sign, he was surprised he could not recall any of the trip after leaving Pelican Street.

He cruised along slowly in Reg's blue 2001 Holden Commodore. Euston Road ran along one side of Sydney Park for nearly one kilometre. The park was over forty hectares with meandering walkways, landscaped gardens and flowing creeks.

Ahead a young man in a white t-shirt was standing near a red Monaro parked on the side of the street. As Max pulled over, Jeremiah crossed the road and ambled into the park. After one hundred metres he sat on a semi-circular timber and cement park bench. A moment later Max joined him. Morning joggers and walkers with their dogs passed the men as they sat facing the rising sun.

'I am hugging you Max,' said Jeremiah as they sat. 'Hard and long and imparting all the goodness I can give you.'

Max looked at him with moistened eyes. He knew Jeremiah found sustained close bodily contact difficult. 'Yes... I feel it,' he cried.

'I know everything now,' nodded the young man. 'It has been a difficult journey. One littered with deceit and betrayal.'

'True.'

'First, I wish to confess. I did steal a mobile phone from your security room. There seemed to be an adequate supply available. And I did deactivate your system completely for the purpose of exchanging vehicles with your nice neighbour, Ted.'

'Thank you for that,' nodded Max.

'It is Laura that led me here. To find this evil.'

'Laura?'

'The magnetic GPS tracker. I secured your birthday present to his undercarriage.' Jeremiah pulled out a phone and showed the screen to Max. A blue circle pulsated mid screen.

'Is he there now?'

'Out cycling. Left an hour ago. I expect he would be returning soon. He is unaware of my presence.'

The men took a quiet moment and looked straight ahead in contemplation. Two female power walkers in matching red Lycra short shorts and orange t-shirts waddled past at pace. Some bubbling noises emanated from the creek only metres away.

'Did you see what he did to her?' asked Max.

Jeremiah nodded, squeezed his eyes closed. Fluid pushed out between his eyelashes. 'And I will utter my judgments against them touching all their wickedness, who have forsaken me, and have burned incense unto other gods, and worshipped the works of their own hand,' he looked to the sky as he spoke. Then he dropped his head. 'There were two marks on her body. He disabled her with a taser. Then he did such things that must not be spoken of.'

'Where did he take her?'

'Nothing good can come from knowing.'

'Jeremiah, where did he take her? Where did he mutilate her?'

He looked at Max. 'The depth of such pain can never be measured. He took Laura to your underground accommodation.'

'Oh God,' gasped Max.

'I most carefully and respectfully retrieved her body from there,' he said. 'It was not for you to find.' Max buried his head in his hands and sobbed. Jeremiah inched closer on the bench. His hand shook as he slowly extended his arm and dropped it over Max's shoulder. The young man gasped as he made physical contact then grimaced as he pulled himself tightly into his friend and joined Max in a profound outpouring of grief. Some passers by slowed and stared but no one stopped.

* * *

It was eight-forty-five when Jeremiah drove Max to a low set home only two blocks from where they had been sitting. Max was astounded when the young man drove the Monaro straight into the driveway and parked outside the double garage doors.

'He has put the Lancer in the garage since I checked earlier this morning. We can expect him to be home,' said Jeremiah. 'He would be unaware that Laura's body is in the boot of his vehicle. Are you ready? Are you enabled?'

'I am stunned and numb. But I am more than capable. What now?'

'I shall go and talk to him.'

'What? Just knock on the door?'

'Yes. Allow twenty seconds after he opens the door. Then press the horn please, Max. Once you see I have secured him I would like for you to move this Monaro a little way down the road.'

'Yeah, okay, I guess,' replied Max unsurely.

Jeremiah grabbed his calico bag, got out and took a few steps towards the front door before turning back and going to the passenger side window of the Monaro.

'Max, to move the vehicle you will need to occupy the driver's seat.'

'Oh, yes. Of course.' Max changed seats.

Jeremiah went to the front door, pressed the doorbell and knocked as well.

The door unlocked and opened as far as the security chain would allow. 'Yes. Can I help you?' said Halliday.

'The Lord Jesus Christ has guided me to your home,' said Jeremiah with a huge smile. 'I am not a collector. I require less than two minutes of your precious time.'

'I am not interested, thank you.' He moved to close the door.

'But sir…stop… for a moment,' he said firmly. Halliday stopped closing the door.

'Hey? What's your story, buster?' he snarled.

'I represent the Church of Vengeance and Justice…' The car horn sounded.

'What the hell.' He peered out the door to the driveway. 'Is that your car?' asked Halliday.

'No sir. It is not. Our church strives to rectify misdeeds and achieve closure…'

'Go and pester someone else.' Halliday undid the chain and opened the door. He pushed past Jeremiah and, while keeping a careful distance, studied the Monaro. It was not a car he knew. Not one of Judd's or O'Donnell's. It could belong to Kushner. Then he remembered something on a map he was sent by text from Jackson Churchill. There was an X and some red writing that said *Monaro here.* There was a sudden daunting feeling that he had just been played, but it was too late. He felt a stabbing pain in his neck as Jeremiah expelled a syringe full of the sedating drug, Midazolam, into his artery. Halliday twisted around and attempted to grab Jeremiah by the throat. The young man ducked low and pushed a shoulder into his stomach then he straightened and stood up with Halliday over his shoulder. The murderer kicked for a couple of seconds before going limp. Jeremiah turned and carried him into the house and threw him on the floor.

Max watched on from the Monaro. 'Bloody hell.' He moved the vehicle as instructed and for some reason he did not know, then did a quick survey of the immediate area. There was no one nearby and the block next door was a vacant allotment. He walked back, picked up the fallen syringe on his way then closed and locked the front door. Jeremiah was pulling Halliday's pants back up after having given him an intramuscular injection.

'The tranquilizing injection of chlorpromazine will buy us a bit more time than the Midazolam,' said the young man. He dropped the second syringe into his calico bag. He took the first syringe from Max and wiped it over then put Halliday's fingerprints on it. Then he passed it to Max. 'You should take this.'

'What for?' Max took it anyway. Jeremiah gave a nod and a grin.

The two friends stood looking down at the man on the floor. A trickle of blood had flowed around his neck from where he was stuck with the needle. His breathing was deep and slow.

'His name is Michael Plunkett,' said Jeremiah.

'What? No...,' said Max, shaking his head. 'This is Charles Halliday. This is the man that molested and killed my son. This is the man that tore Laura apart.'

Jeremiah picked up some documents from the top of a metal framed glass cabinet that was home to some nice-looking wine glasses and goblets. 'Here is his mail, a passport and a plane ticket for tomorrow to Thailand. They are all Plunkett.'

'The bastard has acquired a second identity.' Max took the items and flicked through them. 'Maybe that's something I should've done myself years ago. But this changes nothing.'

'You must trust me, Max.'

'I absolutely do.' He took a step towards him. Jeremiah raised his hands for him not to get too close. The hug earlier was the first he could remember since being a child. One a day would be enough for now. Max stood close but not too close. 'You are the strangest person I have ever met. I don't understand you most of the time.'

'You must take this back.' Jeremiah handed him the mobile he had used for tracking.

'Sure, I don't really need it.

'You might.'

'And I do trust you.' He pocketed the phone. 'I so wish Laura had got to know you.'

Jeremiah looked into Max's eyes. 'And they shall fight against thee; but they shall not prevail against thee; for I *am* with thee, to deliver thee.'

'Well, cool. Sounds good to me,' said Max with the hint of a smile.

'I need to be excused for now.'

'Sure. Off you go.' Max watched as the young man turned and headed down the hallway. He appeared to be going to the bathroom.

Jeremiah turned at the end of the hallway and opened the back door and stepped outside.

As Max sat and sank into a soft lounge chair, he thought he heard a dog barking but then quickly dismissed the thought and looked at Halliday / Plunkett. What to do now? Do I take him to the bunker? Do I tell Heath? Do I wait till he wakes then spend as many days as I can watching him bleed and lose body parts until he dies? The thought of dropping him alive into an acid bath flicked through his mind. He heard a door close. 'Jeremiah! You okay?' There was no reply. He couldn't walk away from Halliday just to see what the guy was up to. Best give him a few minutes.

As many more minutes ticked by, he heard something unexpected. Sirens. Lots of sirens. Max went to the window. 'Holy shit!'

There were police everywhere. By the look of their positions they had quietly arrived and set up vantage points before the sirens sounded. Now they were behind vehicles with weapons at the ready. The house would be surrounded. It looked like both the Australian Federal Police and the state police.

His brain wasn't functioning so well, but there was an unconscious man on the floor and an empty syringe. He tipped over a chair, threw the documents about the room and put a rip in his shirt. Now he could go to the front door. Max unlocked everything. After dropping to his knees, he pulled the door open, placed his hands on his head and hoped no one was trigger happy.

CHAPTER 40

THE INTERVIEW

'I used my GPS tracker and followed him,' said Max. 'I tend to get a bit paranoid when I see the same vehicle repeatedly.'

Maxwell Judd was in an interviewing room, sitting on one of four chairs that were bolted to the floor in front of a table that was similarly attached. The walls were turquoise, and a camera was mounted high in one corner. Opposite him was Senior Sergeant David Heath, in uniform, and Detective Roger Glynn, from the AFP, in a suit and tie. Max was still in his shorts and ripped shirt.

He was not under arrest. More under the threat of arrest unless he decided to talk.

'Somehow you snuck out of your apartment, unseen and attached it to his car?' said Heath.

'I am very stealthy.'

'This is the mobile you used to track the device?' The senior sergeant held up a mobile.

'Yes. I think the app is still open. You can still see it is still operational.'

'Yes.' The blue circle pulsed on the screen. 'I see. Why was he following you?'

'He wanted to kill me before I killed him,' said Max openly. 'Tell me sergeant, have you checked my car yet?' Max was prepared to explain most, but not everything, to Heath and his partner.

'It's senior sergeant. You would already know we have.'

'Then you would already know why I wanted him dead,' replied Max.

The two officers looked at each other.

'We saw the iPad video. Absolutely appalling, and clearly, Halliday was one of the three men.'

'That was my son, Daniel. You did know he was murdered? Right? Friday the fifteenth of November 2013.'

Max went through the story of Walter James Robinson and the DVD which he had copied to his iPad. He went over the shooting of Leonard Campbell which happened while he was still on the force and he confessed to wanting to kill the remaining two men on the video.

'I found Halliday. You and your friends saved his life which is unfortunate. The other monster, Robert Mallory has given me the slip for now. But I will find him too.'

'Really? But you are so stealthy,' said Heath with some sarcasm. 'And this Mallory who is not so bright has given you the slip.'

'Temporarily.'

'How do you think Halliday found you?'

'I am not as invisible as he is… or was. And I think he got some information from a Thailand jail. A guy by the name of Ross Miller.'

'The paedophile ex-cop. I know about him.'

'He was not *ex* when he was busted.'

'You know Mallory's brother, Carl, was murdered?'

'I knew that. Laura told me. It was probably Halliday. Looking for Robert Mallory and not getting the answers he wanted.'

'Laura's body was in his car boot,' said Heath as he studied Max's face.

Max was quiet. He looked down and pushed a hand across his bald head. Yes, her body was there. Her headless and handless body. His eyes filled with water. With thumb and forefinger, he pushed hard on the bridge of his nose. After one minute he raised his head. 'He needs to die.'

'I would agree, but we will have to settle with life in prison. If you killed him, you would have ended doing some time yourself.'

'I would have done that gladly.'

'Hmm…' nodded Heath. 'We have a knife from his place too. Looks like it has some old blood on it. Could be the murder weapon for Carl Mallory.'

'Two life sentences then,' said Max.

'Do you know the other addresses he uses?' asked David Heath.

'One would be Bruce Street.'

'We have sent some officers over. Have you been there?'

'I dropped in and had a nice chat to Mrs Brandis,' said Max. 'I broke into his room… with her permission.'

'And…'

'And… nothing. The room was totally bare. Floor, cupboards, drawers, not a thing.' Max kept the letter to himself. 'Mrs Brandis said he dropped around and collected a large box of belongings.'

'Box of what?'

'Sounded like mostly DVDs. And I'm guessing they weren't

rated G.'

'Did you impersonate a police officer?'

'No. I said I was a detective. Which was completely true.'

Heath tilted his head to the side then gave a shrug of his shoulders as he looked at his colleague who nodded back.

'What do you know about Plunkett?' asked Detective Glynn accepting it was now his turn. Roger Glynn was a strong looking man with a thick crop of black hair behind a receding hairline. His lips were thin and matched a narrow pointy nose.

'All news to me. I knew nothing until I saw his documents, which was not long before you showed up.'

'Have you ever heard the name before?'

'No. Why? Is he famous?'

'Not really. Michael Plunkett was a mercenary over in Yemen. We were alerted less than twenty-four hours ago that a man by that name was being held by police in Yemen for possible passport fraud. Now we know the man they are holding is the *real* Michael Plunket. Your Halliday was given an alternative identity…'

'He's not *my* Halliday by any stretch of the imagination,' interrupted Max.

'Apologies,' said Glynn. 'Halliday had a second identity, all orchestrated by someone who would have thought Plunkett died in Yemen. He was injured… badly. But still very much alive. We want that orchestra conductor.'

'Can't help at all. Sorry.'

'Where's Halliday's phone?'

'Never saw his phone. You guys searched the place.'

'No phone.' Glynn shook his head. 'A computer but no email trail either.'

'I can't help. You'll have to water-board Halliday when he wakes up,' quipped Max.

Glynn was not amused. 'We don't do that sort of thing. Tell me what you injected Halliday with?'

This was a clever question thought Max and a good one to ask a guy who is struggling to think clearly. 'Whatever *he* put in the syringe. I did say he tried to stab me with the thing. We fought. I got hold of the syringe. That's all there is to it.'

'We found some ampoules and plastic syringe packets in the boot with Laura's body,' volunteered Heath. Max reflected on Jeremiah's last biblical quotation of support. His friend was well ahead of the game and he probably took Halliday's phone as well. Although Max could not understand why he would want it.

'He's still unconscious,' continued Health. 'Which makes us think there was something quite potent in the syringe. We should have pathology results soon enough.'

The two police kept Max there another thirty minutes asking mundane questions and repeating others, probably in an attempt to get him to make a mistake. They sent him on his way at lunchtime.

CHAPTER 41

DETONATION

Max got an Uber back to Reg's car parked on Euston Road near Sydney Park. It had been illegally parked since nine, but fortunately had not been towed away. There was a note under the wiper.

Call me – Jeremiah

Max sat in the Commodore with the engine running. He found the number from Jeremiah's call last night and phoned him.

'Hello, Max,' he answered. We need to meet in the clearing at your underground accommodation. This would be a matter of some urgency.'

'I am in your hands,' replied Max. There would be a good reason, and if he stopped to think about it, he would, sooner or later, probably work it out. But now someone else was doing the thinking so he didn't need to. 'I'll be an hour and a half.'

'Change the Commodore for your black van. See you soon. Drive safely.' The call ended.

On the trip he had some vague recollection of cutting a couple of drivers' off, there were some horns. He may have run a red light or two but wasn't sure. Sooner than he realised, he had started driving up the bouncy back road to his property. He slammed on the brakes as he realised he had not changed vehicles. Max reversed and did the circuit back to the house where he swapped to the van.

Back at the rear of his acreage he drove straight over the top of the two gates that were flat on the ground.

As he entered the clearing there was the red Monaro. And there was Jeremiah sitting cross-legged on the bonnet in prayer. He pulled alongside and sat there looking at the shed, knowing that beneath it was where Laura suffered and died.

A knock on his window brought him back to the present. It was Jeremiah. Max let the window down.

'Can I take the van. I have an errand. I will be back within an hour. I only ask one thing of you. Stay above ground while I am gone and when I come back.'

'Sure.'

'Thank you.'

Max just sat there and looked back at the shed.

'Max, you will need to alight from the vehicle.'

'Oh, yes. Sorry.' He got out and sat in the Monaro. Jeremiah left in the van.

*   *   *

An hour later Jeremiah drove past Max and pulled up near the shed. He proceeded to unload drum after drum which he carried through the door, down the stairs and into the bunker. Max just watched. Eventually his job was completed. He moved the van back alongside the Monaro.

The two bald men sat together in the red car.

'I'm going to blow up your underground accommodation,' said Jeremiah.

'I guessed that,' replied Max. 'You smell of petrol and oil.'

'It must be done. Look here.' He pulled out a phone. 'This is the evil one's phone. These are his messages.' He passed the phone over.

Max shook his head as he scrolled through the details. 'So, he was following me. At least for a while.'

'Your plan was working to begin with.'

'Shit. He had a map of my place! How the hell did that happen? And bloody hell, Jeremiah – JC. What's with this? Is there a JC on every fucking corner?'

'They are common enough initials.'

'But to actually call yourself that. Not so common I think. I found out one of Frank Mortimer's guys is Eli Jesus Christensen – otherwise known as JC.'

'Yes, I have met him.'

'What? When?'

'When he, and another man, threw Susan Mortimer over the cliff.'

'I knew you were there, Jeremiah. I saw the phone calls you made and received.'

'Yes. I left the phone for you to find.'

'Oh, yes of course you did,' said Max sarcastically. 'Did they wear black balaclavas?'

'They did.'

'Who was the other man?' asked Max.

'Aloisi.'

'Aloisi who?'

'No idea.'

'What else do you know about him?'

'He is a thirty-two-year-old islander with a short haircut,' replied Jeremiah.

'An islander? Oh, this is too much for me.' Max shook his head. I need some Panadol or maybe something stronger.'

'The JC who sent those messages we can discuss tomorrow.'

'Fine with me,' sighed Max.

'This first,' said Jeremiah as he dipped into his bag. He removed a mosquito coil and a penknife. Carefully he made a hole through part of the coil about three centimetres from the end. He then took two new matches from a box, broke them off near the ends and placed the match heads into the hole. They fitted neatly. He lit the coil and placed it on the small metal stand. 'The evil one, Frank Mortimer and his men, Ian Friend and the other JC all know of this place.'

'I am good with it. Go ahead... oh shit...Ted's car!'

'All taken care of. Returned to its rightful place. Your neighbours are contented. I will position this now.' He left the car and went back to the shed.

*   *   *

Once again, they were both back in the Monaro looking at the green shed.

'Are we far enough back?' asked Max.

'Don't know. Never done this before. We have about another minute before the coil reaches the mat....' There was a massive explosion. The green shed lifted completely off the ground, the door flew clean off and through the air. Fire blasted out in all directions.

The door went straight over the two cars.

'Woo hoo!' shouted Jeremiah. His face lit up with joy like Max had never seen before. This guy really is a lunatic.

The shed collapsed. Fire kept raging. Jeremiah left the Monaro and grabbed an extinguisher from the van and proceeded to put out a few small spot fires in the grass.

CHAPTER 42

JOGGING

After three hours, while there was still some smoke, the fire was out, and the men had returned to the house. The Monaro went in the garage and the van stayed outside.

Jeremiah found the Panadol for Max. In addition, he had dropped up to the bottle shop and came back with a bottle of vodka which he mixed with Max's orange juice. After four strong drinks Max seemed to have finally gone to sleep.

The Bible reader chose to stay awake and keep an eye on things just in case. He knew where the Beretta was if needs be. Not that he had ever used a gun before or even had the need to do so.

*   *   *

Max was up at six-thirty and feeling not too bad for someone that rarely drinks. He and Jeremiah went for a five kilometre planning jog.

Sunrise was at six-forty and the temperature was fourteen degrees – very comfortable for a morning run. New Jerusalem Road was a narrow bitumen route with no guttering and bushland along both sides, except for an occasional driveway and gravel side road. With minimal traffic they could jog side by side.

'For the time being Halliday is out of the way,' said Max. 'The focus must be on the other threat. The counsellor. Do you feel able to tell me things or does the Lord still have your tongue?'

'I am free to converse with you now.'

'That's a refreshing change. Firstly, did you call the police yesterday morning?'

'I was guided by God,' said Jeremiah. 'I had no choice. Were you upset?'

'Surprised. But it worked out okay.'

'I'm glad of that.'

'What about your contact with Ian Friend?' asked Max.

'The counsellor had a role in the killing of Susan Mortimer. It was supposed to be a favour to you,' came the reply. 'That's how he sold it to me. I called him to confirm it had happened.'

'This JC guy works for him?'

'The Eli JC, yes.'

'Okay, one JC at a time please. Eli also works for Frank,' said Max. 'The whole thing smells rotten to me. I haven't been wanting to believe it. But there it is staring me in the face.'

'You're thinking that Ian Friend runs a major drug distribution network? And Eli Jesus Christensen is his undercover agent?'

'Yes. Setting off smoke bombs and stealing Frank's product. Trying to undermine his drug business. Yes, it's the only logical conclusion.' added Max. 'Am I right?'

'The counsellor is very careful. Always hands off. I am not his confidante. I cannot give you the answer you seek.'

The two joggers moved off to the side as a tradesman's ute sped by.

'I don't believe he would kill you himself,' said Jeremiah.

'I reckon that's true. But he is more than happy to set the wheels in motion for someone else to do it for him.'

'It's his fault Laura is dead.'

'Is it?' Max was a little thrown by the comment and slowed to a walk. 'Hey, slow down.' He ran forward a few paces and tapped Jeremiah on the shoulder. 'What do you mean it was his fault?'

'Think it through, Max. What if Frank wasn't after you two days ago?'

'I guess my plan for Halliday would not have been disrupted.'

'Halliday would be on your bench and Laura would be alive,' said Jeremiah. 'And then there's the map.'

'And Frank was only after me because the counsellor sent him the map via JC Eli.' Max stopped and bent over with his hands on his knees and screamed as loud as he could. It seemed to help. He stood back up.

'Ian Friend is a killer by proxy, Max,' said Jeremiah.

'And he knew I had leads to finding Halliday.'

'Perfect timing or just coincidence?'

Max put a hand on Jeremiah's shoulder then quickly pulled it away realising what he was doing. 'Sorry.'

'It's okay,' nodded Jeremiah. 'Just so you know. I will have nothing further to do with the counsellor.'

'Good. Now let's run faster.' They were nearly halfway so they turned and headed back at pace.

CHAPTER 43

BACON & EGGS

Back at the rear of the Oakdale house, overlooking the duck pond, Max and Jeremiah sat down to a breakfast of bacon and eggs with orange juice.

'Do you know where I may get hold of a car cover. Not a new one,' asked Max.

'Your neighbour,' replied Jeremiah immediately. 'Should I visit him again?'

'Might be best if I go this time.'

'Okay.'

'I have an idea as to how I might be able to sort some of this mess.'

'Great to hear.' Jeremiah was devouring his bacon with the soft poached eggs.

'We will need to be cautious.'

'Yes.'

Max looked at him as he ate. Anyone else would be asking questions right now. 'Aren't you even going to ask what the plan is?'

'Why? You seem very enabled now.'

'I have moved on from despair with help from you, yes.'

'These farm eggs are superb.'

'Jeremiah...' said Max. He took a sip of coffee before continuing. His friend looked up. 'Ian Friend. Did he give you the drugs that were found scattered around Quentin's body?'

'Indirectly. They were Frank's originally. I guess they went back to the Mortimers in the end.'

'JC stole them?'

'Yes. With help.'

'From you?' asked Max.

'No. Gail and Alex. Two addicts.'

'He used you and he used others to undermine the Mortimers.'

'He counselled and instructed me into believing I was doing the right thing, helping others. Particularly you,' said Jeremiah through a mouthful of food.

'I know all about the Jedi mind control tricks,' said Max. 'The hypnosis he uses. What a bastard.'

'I *was* like a lamb *or* an ox *that* is brought to the slaughter; and I knew not that they had devised devices against me, *saying*, Let us destroy the tree with the fruit thereof, and let us cut him off from the land of the living, that his name may be no more remembered.'

'The book of Jeremiah?'

'Yes.'

'To me you will never be forgotten,' said Max. 'You are a true friend and a wonderful human being.'

'Do you have any more bacon?'

CHAPTER 44

THE PLAN

Around midnight Max had spent time cleaning and wiping down surfaces inside and outside the Monaro. He wasn't really expecting it to land in the hands of the police, but he wasn't taking any chances.

At two o'clock in the morning he drove the car slowly up Kareela Road in the upmarket suburb of Cremorne Point. He parked alongside a wooden railing that overlooked the waterway and boat access to Sydney Harbour. Before he left the car, he took an, *Ian Friend: Psychologist: Hastings Psychology*, business card from his wallet and dropped it on the floor. After grabbing the car cover from the passenger seat, he hopped out as quietly as he could and set about securing it to the Monaro.

Five minutes later he walked away, and after one kilometre, in Murdoch Street, hopped into the black van driven by Jeremiah.

Everything for part one of the plan had gone fine but nevertheless Max felt nauseated. He was potentially setting up someone he had trusted and confided in for years to be killed, or at the very least seriously harmed. A person that had been of tremendous support at the most difficult of times – generous with his time and money. And a person who had tried to have him murdered. A person that had lied and deceived him and a person who had undoubtedly caused incalculable harm to so many through drug dealing. Ian Friend had become wealthy at the expense of others.

Let's see him hypnotise his way out of this one. Max nodded to himself at the thought. He had partially reassured himself.

*   *   *

At nine-thirty he rang Reg and apologised for not having returned his car and said he would need it for a little longer. He gave the Courtesy Officer an update on Halliday's arrest.

At ten in the morning Max made his next call.

'Hello,' answered Frank.

'Frank, this is Max Judd. We need to meet.'

'You looking for work?'

'No. I have information that will interest you. Probably best it is just you and me, face to face. You have a mole on your payroll.'

'Do I?'

'There is no doubt. Are you okay to meet me alone? Lunch somewhere?'

'You not planning a hit on me, are you?' he laughed.

'Not my style, Frank.'

'Yes, yes I know that Judd. Otto on the wharf in three hours. But only if you let me buy you lunch.'

'See you there.'

The call ended.

'I'm meeting him for lunch down at the wharf,' said Max.

'I'm not invited?' asked Jeremiah.

Max pondered the thought of taking along the man that ripped Frank's son throat out with his teeth. 'I don't think the menu would suit you,' he said with a smile.

'What time do you expect to return?'

'Three, maybe three thirty. Is this important?'

'I have something to show you,' said Jeremiah with absolutely no change in his bland demeanour. 'That time frame will be adequate.'

'Do you wish to enlighten me any further?'

'No.'

'Okay,' Max let out a big sigh. 'A surprise awaits. Lord knows!'

'Yes, he does.'

*   *   *

Max put on a brown suit jacket over a white open neck shirt and some stretch grey denim jeans. He drove off in Reg's car for a seventy-minute trip.

The Wharf at Woolloomooloo in Sydney juts out four-hundred metres into Sydney Cove. On one side is a marina and the other the naval shipyards. Otto Ristorante faces the marina and the Royal Botanical Gardens, beyond this is the city skyline.

The alfresco area looked refined and pristine with many square tables covered in white table cloths with white folded cloth napkins, fine cutlery and glassware. Some tables were moved together to accommodate more diners or in this case just one, Frank Mortimer. He sat on his own, well away from other patrons. The jacket of his three-piece wool suit was over the back of his chair. He was sipping red wine.

The waiter approached Max as he arrived.

'I'm with Frank,' said Max and nodded his head in the direction of the curly haired godfather.

'Very good, sir.'

He sat opposite.

'This is the life, Judd. Food, wine and there's my beautiful cruiser just moored over there.' Frank raised his glass. 'Care for a glass?'

'I'm driving. I'll stick with water for now.'

'Suit yourself.' He poured some shiraz down his throat. 'I think we should order first. We're not in any rush, are we?'

'No rush. What do you recommend, Frank?'

'The pepper seared Hiramasa Kingfish for main. The peach semifreddo with fresh peach and balsamic for dessert.'

'Sounds delicious. I'll go for that.'

'You won't be sorry.' Frank waved a hand.

The waiter arrived. Filled up Frank's wine and took the order.

The two men chatted about numerous things. Fishing, in which Max had little interest; Donald Trump and fake news, in which he had even less interest; the subject of motorcycles got him singing the praises of his Harley Davidson Road King and this then inevitably led to cars and then to the red Monaro.

'Someone has been feeding me poor intel about the car. What did they hope to gain?' asked Frank.

'I'd just be guessing. It was a sure way to get you out there so you could see my bunker and glean what I was up to. Make some incorrect connection with Quentin and somehow implicate me in his death. And maybe throw you off other lines of enquiry, Frank.'

The kingfish arrived. It was cut beautifully in thick slices, lightly seared on the outside and with a crust of black pepper and sitting upright on a bed of fried green tomatoes. A chilli, lime and cucumber dressing was drizzled over the top and in a wide arc around the over-sized plate.

'Buon appetito,' said Frank. Max raised his water.

Apart from oohs and aahs and some nods of pleasure over the food, proper conversation had ceased temporarily.

As Frank used his finger to mop up the last of the dressing he asked, 'You say I have a mole in my employ. How would you know this?' He sucked his finger.

'I have some very reliable sources and after your impromptu visit I needed to do some homework. I know who JC is.'

'Let's say this is true. Why tell me? What's in this for you, Judd?'

'I assume you have some friends on the inside. In prison. People you can trust?'

'I have a wide network,' said Frank as a waiter arrived and cleared the empty plates.

'The third man in the iPad video. He has been arrested. He murdered a police woman and the brother of one of his past associates.'

'Would that be the police woman you were seeing.'

Max took a breath and briefly closed his eyes. Of course, Frank would know this. 'Yes,' he replied. 'It was extremely brutal.'

'Like Quentin?' said Frank blandly. He sipped his wine.

'To me. So much worse than Quentin.'

'And he assaulted and murdered your son.' Frank padded his

mouth with a serviette. Max just nodded. 'You want some prison justice in exchange for information?' continued Frank.

'I do.'

'If what you tell me turns out to be accurate, we will have a deal.'

'He will be in remand until his trial. Probably at Silverwater,' said Max.

'What would you like to happen?'

Max looked at Frank. 'I want him to suffer…daily. Pain, assault, penetration. Not enough to send him to hospital. For at least a month before he dies. And I want you to keep me updated.'

'Hospital or not. The process could continue,' smiled Frank. 'Who is my mole?'

'Eli.'

'Yeah?' Frank gave a slight raise of his eyebrows.

'His full name is Eli Jesus Christensen. Known to some people as JC. He was given the map by a psychologist, Ian Friend. Friend and I have some history together. He would send me referrals for my community service business. I have questioned him, perhaps once too often, about his expanding property portfolio.' As Max dropped the name of his counsellor it jarred him inside. He had considered not providing it, but this would be both pointless and risky as Frank would inevitably find out.

'Good, Max. And you think this Friend, is the one who is trying to cut in on my business?'

'That's for you to determine. I won't be having contact with him again. But it seems a very logical explanation for recent events involving us both, Frank.'

The dessert arrived. A generous orange mouse like serving topped with sliced peaches and set amongst lines of peach balsamic vinegar. They both tucked in.

CHAPTER 45

CHURCHILL

Max arrived back at Oakdale at three-thirty. He found Jeremiah out the back sitting on a boulder feeding bread to the ducks.

'The three colourful ones are mandarins,' announced Max. 'Fatso, Stretch and Stinkie. The rest are wood ducks.'

'They have quite a few offspring,' said Jeremiah.

'They do. Might be getting too many for the pond.' Max sat down next to his friend.

'Your kids would love this.'

'They do. But it's all going soon. Well, at least I will be. Friend owns this property. I need to clear out.'

'Where to?'

'Don't know yet. Maybe back to Melbourne. Still have a place down there. I gotta talk to Claire.'

'Pelican Street is definitely out.' Jeremiah threw a crust high in the air and caused some excitement in the pond.

'It is. Claire wanted to sell it anyway. That would be best.'

They both watched the ducks frantically searching for more bread.'

'Which mandarin is which?' asked Jeremiah.

'No idea. The kids know.' Max turned to him. 'You have some surprise for me?'

'I do. We should go to the garage.'

'The garage eh! I am intrigued. Lead the way.'

They walked down the side of the home and round to the front. Jeremiah pressed the remote and the garage door opened. There was the black van and the Harley and a space for another vehicle. Reg's car was parked in the driveway.

'Yes?' said Max.

Jeremiah lifted the rear door of the van. Down either side was a narrow bench seat and behind the front seats a large laundry basket with cushions on the top of water bottles, and sealed packets of confectionary and biscuits. A man was lying on the floor in a star shape. There were handcuffs on each of his ankles and wrists which were chained to the underside of the seats. The right side of his bearded face was purple and swollen. An intravenous line was connected to his right arm with a bag of saline held up by a hook into an air vent.

'Oh Jesus!' yelled Max at the same time covering his nose.

'No, Jesus is the other JC. This is Jackson Churchill,' said Jeremiah.

'What the hell, Jeremiah?'

'This man was communicating with Plunkett or Halliday.'

'What have you done to him?'

'He had a car accident. He is sedated.'

'With what?'

'I did secure some of your items before we blew the shed.'

'Not just the drugs I see.'

'I put Sublimaze in the saline bag.'

'Shit, that's a very potent narcotic. What dose are you giving him?'

'No idea,' said Jeremiah. 'But I have kept an eye on him, and it seems adequate.'

Max moved closer. There were towels under Churchill's backside that were wet and stinking of urine.

'How long has he been here?'

'Couple of days.'

'You've used my good beach towel.'

'Sorry.'

Churchill's breathing was shallow but his colour, outside of his right cheek, looked good. There was something about his left hand. Max hopped into the van. 'Did you bite his index finger off?'

Jeremiah, or at least Ezekiel, had a clear history of such acts. This was the first one Max knew of since he had resurfaced in Sydney.

'I cauterised it with the paint burner,' said Jeremiah. 'He is not yet forgiven.'

'Bloody hell. Where was I when you were doing all this?'

'You were intoxicated and sleeping. Although it started back at Plunkett's house…'

On Monday morning at Rooty Hill…

As Jeremiah moved into the backyard of Plunkett's house a phone in his pocket started vibrating and barking. There was a text message…

My contact has advised that MJ is unscathed from the visit by FM. Do you wish to engage me any further in this matter? As you know I can escalate my services to meet your requirements. Please advise.

JC

As Jeremiah made his way around the property and to the Monaro, he placed a call to triple zero.

You have dialed emergency triple zero. Your call is being connected… Came the voice from the phone.

Ten seconds later a female voice asked. 'Police, fire or ambulance?'

'Police,' he said.

'What state and town is the emergency in?'

'Rooty Hill. New South Wales.'

'Connecting police now,' said the lady.

A few seconds later there was a man's voice asking for the address. Jeremiah spoke firmly and loudly told him the Rooty Hill address and then said, 'This is where Michael Plunkett lives and where you will find the body of Detective Laura O'Donnell.' He disconnected the call.

Once in the Monaro he went back to the text message and replied.

I will require your assistance. Can we meet tonight. 9 pm. Rear access way as per the map you sent. Security is down. MJ is alone on the property. MP

A minute later there was a reply.

I'll be there and will phone you on my arrival. You must answer to confirm our plans. JC

Jeremiah sent back a thumbs-up emoji. Then he switched off the phone, removed the SIM card and drove back to Oakdale.

*   *   *

By eight o'clock on Monday evening Max had finished the fourth screwdriver and was fading fast.

'You should retire now,' said Jeremiah. Max was on the recliner. He took a deep breath and stretched. 'Go to bed, Max. You need it.'

'Yes. I will. Thank you.' Max dragged himself vertical and staggered off in the direction of his bedroom. A few minutes later the toilet flushed, and soon after, the bedroom light went out.

The young man sat cross legged on the sofa praying quietly for a further ten minutes. Then he was up. First to the currently defunct security room where he tucked the Beretta into his shorts. Then to the shed out the back where he grabbed an axe and finally to the kitchen for the van keys.

Jeremiah drove the circuit to the rear of the property.

In the headlights he could see the twisted mess that was once a garden shed and underground bunker. Two narrow columns of grey smoke snaked out of the ruins and disappeared above the light beams. He turned on the mobile and reinserted the SIM card.

He secured one end of a nylon cord to a twisted piece of burnt aluminium that was partly obscured by another. The other end he tied to a torch. He stood the mobile against a rock on the ground.

Jeremiah drove the van into the bush and out of sight. He grabbed the axe and moved back to the clearing and waited.

At one minute to nine the lights of an approaching vehicle flicked up and down through the trees. Jeremiah turned on the torch and gave it a push so it was swinging back and forth and casting light and shadows around the shed ruins.

Jackson Churchill turned cautiously into the cleared area. He saw the burnt out shed and noticed the movement of light. 'What are you up to Charles?' He leaned forward to the windscreen trying to see who was out there with a torch. Churchill stopped his car fifty metres back, flicked up the high beam then made a phone call. On the ground ahead of him a mobile lit up. 'What the fuck! Where are you?'

His driver's side window suddenly let out a huge bang as it exploded into a thousand pieces. The blunt end of an axe struck him in the side of his face smashing his cheek bone and sending his head and upper body sideways. Despite the injury, Jackson planted his foot and the land cruiser shot forward throwing dirt out behind. He narrowly avoided crashing into the remains of the shed. The car slid around in a tight circle and was heading back to the entrance road. Then the axe came flying into the windscreen. The car veered to the side and crashed into a tree. Jackson was thrown forward. As he reached for the gear stick there was a torch light and the end of a Beretta sticking through the window.

'Choose life or death!' shouted Jeremiah.

CHAPTER 46

CAMDEN

Max threw on a long grey wig, a cap and glasses and drove Reg's car to Camden. He had Churchill lying down on the back seat with his hands handcuffed behind his back just in case. The drip had been removed. The man had moaned and groaned a little but remained quite sedated.

Camden Hospital was the closest ED to Oakdale and only a twenty-minute drive, not that Max was dropping him directly there. The less people he had to see or be seen by the better and avoiding any CCTV cameras would avoid complications. Murrandah Avenue was barely two minutes from the hospital. Max pulled over and placed a call to emergency services. He said a pedestrian had been hit by a car in Murrandah Avenue and was seriously injured and needed an ambulance immediately. He hung up and waited. It only took a minute to hear the siren wailing. Max uncuffed Jackson Churchill, dragged him onto the footpath and fled the scene.

As he made his way back to Oakdale, he placed a call to the police station at Parramatta via their 1300 number and asked for David Heath. When they put him on hold, he pulled over and waited.

'This is Heath,' snapped the Senior Sergeant.

'This is Max Judd.'

'Hello. Any more confessions?'

'Is Glynn still around?'

'He's in a meeting.'

'Tell him that a friend of a friend has informed me that the orchestra conductor has just been admitted to Camden Hospital. His name is Jackson Churchill. Thank you, sergeant.'

'It's senior sergean…'

Max hung up. Switched off the phone. He removed the SIM card and was about to destroy it then changed his mind. 'What the hell. It matters little now.' He put the card back in and continued the drive home.

CHAPTER 47

ANTICIPATION

Early Sunday afternoon Max drove to Pelican Street. He took the elevator to level seven, never really intending to enter 701, a decision that was made easier by it still being under police seal. He stayed there in the foyer for five minutes, pacing back and forth and looking at the door and the police notice before heading down to level one. Reg was at home in 101 and pleased to have his car returned. The Camry had been given the all clear and had been kindly returned to the apartment carpark. Max did wonder if Reg might receive some traffic infringement notices in the mail, but for now he kept quiet about it.

He spent a few minutes with Loretta and Reg and enjoyed a couple of French almond macaroons. The two ex-police officers chatted briefly about some recent events and the arrest of Halliday before Max excused himself saying he had an appointment to meet with Claire. Reg wished him luck. They shook hands and he left.

*　　　*　　　*

The visit to Claire was probably a day or two later than it could have been. Max had made excuses for himself and started the packing up process at Oakdale. He parked his Camry behind Claire's Prius outside the Fergie Street address at St Leonards.

He could see Mavis and Arnie, Claire's elderly parents, further up the street going for a slow walk. This was not a good sign. They had been shuffled off at the scheduled time of his arrival. The chance of fireworks seemed high.

Claire would know from the news reports that Laura had been murdered, her body found at Rooty Hill and a man had been arrested. She would know little else.

Max checked himself in the sun visor mirror and ran a hand around his chin. After he stretched his arms and cracked his knuckles, he took two big breaths and left the partial security of his car.

He opened a low metal gate that he could have stepped over and followed the cement path to the two steps onto the front verandah. As he took his first step towards the door it opened. Claire was in blue denim jeans, sneakers and a faded red t-shirt with *Kevin 07* on the front. She looked good in anything. They both stood there looking at each other saying nothing. Max felt his eyes becoming moist.

'Your hair is a shade darker,' he managed to say through a part smile. 'I like it.'

Her lips quivered. Then she almost leapt across the three metres between them, threw her arms around him and squeezed him harder than she ever had before. She pushed her face against his neck. He could feel her quiet tears on his skin.

Then Max started making some uncontrollable guttural and gagging noises. He wanted to speak but no words would come. His legs went to jelly, and he dropped to his knees leaving Claire standing above and in front of him. He erupted into a loud wailing with tears pouring down his cheeks. A dog across the street started barking. She grabbed his head and pulled it hard against her tummy.

'My poor man,' she whispered. 'My poor, poor man.' She held him tight with one hand and stroked his bald head with the other. Tears streamed down her face, but she made no sound.

After minutes of holding and caressing, Claire said, 'Let's go inside.' Max managed to regain his feet. 'Look at the two of us,' she said wiping her thumbs under his eyes. 'People made of nails have turned soft as butter. What's the good of that. Come on.' She took his hand and they went inside.

The house was dated and the furniture old but functional. The lounge chairs were a floral pattern with large pale red and orange daisies over a cream background. The sofa and foot stools all matched.

Claire sat Max on a single lounge chair then sat on his knees and curled up on him with an arm around his shoulders and her head against his chest.

Finally, he managed a few words. 'It's all over now… everything…completely…permanently.'

'You've paid a big price, Max.' She kissed his cheek. 'I'm so sorry about Laura. I never really got to know her. I didn't give her the time I should have.'

'There was so much going on. I lost control,' sniffed Max. 'I have to live with the consequences.'

'What about her family?'

'They're coming over from Ireland for the funeral on Friday.

Not sure I can handle that.'

'Police face risks every day, Max.'

'Spending time with me seems riskier. You would know that better than anyone.'

'The only person responsible here is Halliday,' said Claire. 'Not you or anyone else.'

'Not just him. There are others. And your hunches were right. I need to tell you about Ian Friend and other things.'

Max told Claire everything about the counsellor. The drugs. The JC confusion. The security double agent, Eli and about the raid by Frank Mortimer and subsequent more amicable lunch. He gave her all the details about the red Monaro and how Jeremiah had helped, then he described the blowing up of the bunker. He even told her about Churchill chained in the van. He went over his meeting with Halliday at Rooty Hill and the police bust and interview.

Part way through the lengthy dialogue Claire had paused him and gone to the kitchen and returned with a bottle of red wine. Max gladly accepted a glass.

The two were now sitting opposite each other in the lounge. Claire topped up both glasses. 'The man I saw here. In the straw hat and sunnies.'

'Halliday,' said Max. 'Reg described him exactly the same at the apartment.'

'The police that were outside said a man had been caught and they did not need to remain any longer. But was he planning to take me?'

'Probably.'

'To kill me?'

'Yes. I think that would have been his plan,' said Max bluntly.

'It was me or Laura. Right?'

'I think he would have liked to get his hands on both of you.'

'Killing Laura hurts you more because he knew you were in an intimate relationship with her.'

Max looked at Claire unsure how to respond.

'It's okay,' she continued. 'I knew. I could tell when I was there on your birthday. I have a good radar for these things. I knew when you had sex with that Angel gym woman, and I knew you were with Laura. Let's not pretend.'

Max had argued the point about sex with Angel many months ago. While he never had intercourse with her, his fingers, with Angel's direction, did find their way into her vagina. It was a means to an end that was all. And with Laura they had not had sex at all until after his birthday. However, he knew he had no argument here. The best he could do was say nothing or agree.

'I think Halliday and his friend, Churchill, knew about me and Laura. Once he got the message that Frank Mortimer was on my tail, he changed his plans, and everything turned to shit.'

Claire nodded and took up her glass. 'Where do we go from here?'

'I have been asking myself the same question. Is it ever possible we may live together again? One day. Sometime. Weeks, months or longer.'

'You've really given everything up? One hundred percent?'

'Yes. The bunker is destroyed.'

'Bunker or no bunker. That means shit, Max.'

'No, it's over. No more vigilante.' Max shook his head. 'I need to find a job. Probably some more legitimate security work. Shopping centres, music concerts, festivals that sort of thing.'

'I need to think it over.'

'Okay. That's a start. And I think what you said about selling Pelican Street was right. You should move on. We should both move on from that.'

'I thought you wanted me to keep it.'

'No. I've thought about it and I'm happy for it to go.'

'Because I was having second thoughts about selling.'

'You have bad memories from there. We both do. You must sell it, Claire,' insisted Max.

'Must? Why? Is there something else I should know?'

Max jumped up. 'Oh, God!' He paced the small room. He grabbed his ears and started over-breathing.

'Max!'

'Oh God! Oh God!'

*   *   *

It took an hour and another bottle of red, but Max eventually told Claire every detail of Laura's grisly death right down to Grandmas blue willow plate.

She agreed to sell.

CHAPTER 48

CHRIST THE REDEEMER

When Jeremiah was Ezekiel and last in Sydney on a biting rampage, Max had managed to work out the bizarre code he was using. All his attacks occurred in a range of locations. The beginning letter of which spelt out a religious message.

Ingleburn; Artarmon; Merrylands; Kingsford; Illawong; Neutral Bay; Granville; Ingleside; Auburn; Manly; Gosford; Oatley; Double Bay; Cecil Hills

I A M K I N G I A M G O D C – I am King. I am God. C...

At the time he had wondered where the "C" was heading and had asked Ezekiel...

'The C thing. Indulge me with your guesses.'

'Hmm... Christ the Redeemer? Just off the top of my head. I don't really know,' replied Ezekiel.

'Wow! That's a lot of bites,' said Max.

'Just a guess. The time frame may be years. Who knows?'

It seemed a silly thought, but one that had preoccupied Max's mind as he filled yet another packing carton at his Oakdale home. Jeremiah had bitten off Churchill's finger here at Oakdale. The letter O.

He stacked the carton on another. That made thirty so far. Maybe another ten to go. His hairless friend was out running somewhere. Possibly taking a chunk out of someone else. Who knows? He had been gone for the last six hours, since seven in the morning.

It had been five days since he dropped off Churchill and had lunch with Frank. There had been no further news. Max took this as a good sign. No bodies washed up on the beach. No corpses found in dark alleyways. Yesterday with Claire had been difficult and draining and the outcome for their future remained in limbo but not without hope. She still wanted to be around with his kids whenever they visited, not that there was anywhere for them to visit at the moment. Going forward there was the smallest ray of hope, and that would have to do for now.

An hour later Jeremiah walked back in. Max had left the door unlocked and had tried to make himself feel okay about doing so. He was trying to make some changes.

The young man hardly had any sweat for his outing and was not at all puffed.

'Was that enjoyable?' asked Max.

'Very.'

'How far did you manage?'

'About fifty I think.'

'Did you get hungry on the way?' smiled Max unable to restrain himself.

'I devoured the word of the Lord,' said Jeremiah immediately and grinned back.

'You know you've made a big mistake?' said Max. He opened and taped up another new carton ready to fill.

'Only one?'

'Your code. Christ the Redeemer.'

'Not sure where you are going with this one,' said Jeremiah.

'The last biting, to the best of my knowledge, was here at Oakdale. There is no letter O in Christ the Redeemer.' Max gave him a head tilt and a wink. 'Got ya!'

'Ah, you refer to a conversation from some months ago.'

'See, you do remember.'

'That was just a possibility. It was not clear to me at the time.'

'Where was the previous occasion then? Before here.'

'That would have been in Melbourne at...' Jeremiah thought about it '...at Ivanhoe.'

'Before that?'

'Max, now you're testing me. But I think Vermont and prior to that Ashburton.'

'A V I O... is that anything?'

'If I think it over Max, it's taking the shape of Christ the Saviour.'

Max stopped packing and looked at Jeremiah who gave him a broad smile. 'Two to go!' giggled the young man.

Max started laughing. A moment later they were both laughing.

CHAPTER 49

CATCH UPS

On Tuesday Max received a telephone call from Senior Sergeant David Heath. To begin with he was friendly enough and enquiring about Max's health and recovery from recent ordeals. It wasn't too long before he got onto the subject of Jackson Churchill. Asking who had assaulted and drugged him and dropped him by the roadside.

'This roadside dump of an injured person is strikingly similar to that of one John Watson, who ended up dead. Fortunately, Churchill will recover,' Heath said.

Max stuck to his story of friend of a friend having contacted him despite it sounding lame and contrived.

During the conversation the senior sergeant revealed that the DNA on the knife found at Halliday's Rooty Hill home was that of Carl Mallory. He said that they had interviewed Halliday who had no memory whatsoever of being injected with any drug or indeed having had a fight with Judd or anyone else. This was probably a good thing thought Max. Loss of memory is a very common effect from the drug Midazolam. He thought of Jeremiah and of his selection of medication for both Halliday and Churchill. Obviously, the Lord had uploaded some useful medical information to his brain.

'Halliday is not confessing to Laura's murder, said Heath. 'Despite the remainder of her body being found in the car boot at his residence. And she was not murdered at your unit, at the Rooty Hill home or in the vehicle.'

'He has another place somewhere,' said Max. 'That's where that box of DVD's would be. That's the place you should be looking for.' It was likely there was another place. The DVD's had not been found. And it seemed reasonable to send Heath elsewhere looking for the murder location. Max had plans to bulldoze the area where his shed was and level the ground.

Eventually, Health got around to the other point of his call. He had been contacted by Laura's father. The family would be flying in tomorrow. It was agreed that Max should collect them from the airport and drop them off at an Airbnb.

*   *   *

It was Wednesday and not so long ago he was standing at the very same location disguised as Walter Rowbottom waiting for Halliday. The man he waited for then was, sadly, the reason he was there again now.

There was no mistaking the O'Donnells as they emerged. And it was clear that Laura's father had not contributed a lot to the genetics of Laura's appearance. Mum looked exactly like an older version of Laura and a quick *what could have been* flicked through Max's mind. He greeted the parents, brother and sister with big hugs. There were a lot of polite friendly smiles and a few tears.

The meeting was something he had been dreading, but it seemed the right thing to do, rather than meeting them for the first time at the funeral in two days. He was glad Heath had offered him the opportunity.

He apologised for not being able to offer them accommodation, apart from being a long way out of town, he was on the verge of moving house and packing boxes were everywhere.

The reception he received was one of warmth, kindness and sympathy which was different to the various scenarios he had imagined, and he was pleased he had not, as far as he could tell, ended up on an IRA hit list. He expressed his sincere condolences to all of them and it was clear that he meant every word he was saying.

The conversation in the car was minimal and mostly about Sydney, Australia and the weather. He showed them the nearest shopping centre before dropping them off at their Airbnb in Rockdale which was only a few minutes from the Banksia funeral home.

They insisted he return for dinner that evening. He agreed.

*   *   *

It had been a week since lunch with Frank when Max dropped the names of Eli Jesus Christensen and Ian Friend, but there was still no word from anyone. As he was already in town, a quick visit to Hastings Psychology near Hyde Park seemed worthwhile, just to check for any potential developments.

It was afternoon and Ian would normally schedule appointments on the hour and sometimes on the half hour. Apart from Max's last visit, the counsellor always ran on time. Max decided to arrive there at two-fifteen thus reducing the chance of any contact with Ian if he was there.

Silvia's eyes lit up when she saw him.

'Hey you,' she said warmly. 'How did you go with your detective work?' Max had visited Silvia at her home on the day Laura was murdered. But she knew little of any of that. She could've seen the news reports, but Max's name had not appeared anywhere.

'It was a difficult day. Some things have since been sorted,' replied Max.

'You were a bit on edge.'

'Sorry for being rude.'

'Ian's not here in case you were looking for him,' said Silvia.

'When will he be back?'

'No one seems to know. He left a hand-written note on my desk a few days back. Just said, *Gone fishing, cancel all my appointments* and signed Ian F.'

'His writing?'

'Definitely. But I never knew he even liked fishing. Can't get hold of his wife or son either.'

'Oh, dear,' said Max. He suddenly had an awful sinking feeling and pangs of guilt. Had the whole family been put to the sword by Frank Mortimer? 'Are they like officially missing persons? Is it a police matter?' enquired Max without wanting to sound too dramatic.

'I don't think so. I did call the police to see if there was anything I should do. They called me back a few hours later and said the family is safe and well and there is no cause for concern.'

'That's it?'

'Yep. The officer was quite rude to me.'

'Has anyone else come in here asking about him? Anyone

different to the usual crowd that is?'

'There was some fat guy from the office of Liquor and Gaming asking to see Ian on an *official matter*,' said Silvia indicating quotation marks with her fingers. 'Had ID. Seemed legit.'

'Interesting,' replied Max as calmly as he could. He thought he felt his heart miss a beat or two.

'I was thinking they could've gone overseas on a holiday. Ian did travel from time to time. Maybe there was a sick relative or something. So, no appointments for you Maxwell Judd, which means you will have some spare time to take me to that dinner you owe me!'

'I haven't forgotten, and I do have your number.'

'But I don't have yours.' She flashed a big smile and leant as far over the reception desk as she could showing off a generous cleavage.

'I must be off.' Max took a step back. 'I'll call you.'

'You better!' she said loudly as he made a hasty exit. 'You better, you gorgeous bastard,' she continued after he was gone.

*   *   *

As he headed back to Oakdale, Max was in a state of complete confusion. Was the racing thing real after all? Were the Friend family all dead? How many more miscalculations could he make?

His phone rang. He pushed the green phone icon on the dash and answered hands free.

'Yes,' he said.

'Hello Max. Are we free to talk?' It was Frank Mortimer.

'I'm driving. Alone and hands free.'

'Glad you're not misbehaving.'

'I was wondering what was going on,' said Max.

'Yes. I though that may be the case. All is well. I have corroborated your information. As a bonus I have my Monaro back.'

'Wonderful,' said Max now waiting for the worst news.

'Unfortunately, the people you told me about have gone into hiding. But I will find them,' said Frank calmly.

Max breathed a sigh of relief then tried to sound concerned for Frank. 'That's disappointing.'

'Yes. They were tipped off,' said Mortimer.

Max felt a bit unsure whether this was a statement or a question. 'Hold up there, Frank. Please don't think I had anything to do with that.'

'You can settle, Max. I know who it was. And I have rectified the problem. It was one of my boys. Marco. He was a good man, but there seems to be this ridiculous loyalty code between some security personnel. Marco tipped off Eli and then Eli tipped off Friend. And here we are. That's all fine and that's now my problem, but your information was good and so our deal is in place.'

'Thank you, Frank. Halliday is still in remand awaiting trial.'

'Doesn't matter where he is. He is already finding life behind bars more challenging than he would have ever expected.'

'I appreciate your assistance with the matter.'

'It's possible he could end up at hospital more than once, but as I told you that changes nothing.'

'Good.'

'That's all, Max. The job offer still stands. You have my number.'

'Thanks for the considerat...' the phone beeped. Frank had hung up.

*   *   *

As Max pulled up in the driveway Jeremiah walked out the front door. He had a backpack on and some running shoes.

Max parked the Camry out front. 'Hey. Looks like you're heading off for a big one today.'

'Yes, Max. Visiting an old acquaintance.'

'Really! Will he or she be expecting you?'

'I would think that unlikely.'

'Anyone I know?'

'Enzo Scortini.'

'I feel I should know that name.'

'An underling of Franks. We met once before in Gosford.'

'Ah, the psych ward!'

'Correct. Today he will be forgiven.'

'Lovely. And where does Mister Scortini live?'

'Ultimo. The inner-city area.'

'So that would be "U" then.'

'Your spelling is astounding,' smiled Jeremiah.

'I can drive you. It's a bloody long way from here.'

'The Lord will guide me. But thank you for the offer.'

'After this you will just have "R" and your work will be complete. You can retire!' laughed Max.

'The spoilers are come upon all high places through the

wilderness: for the sword of the LORD shall devour from the *one* end of the land even to the *other* end of the land: no flesh shall have peace.'

'That doesn't sound like any sort of retirement plan to me.'

'Goodbye, Max.'

Jeremiah left, jogging slowly down the driveway.

'Goodbye my friend.' He watched him leave the property, turn onto the road and disappear. Max blotted a tear from his eye.

CHAPTER 50

THE GREATEST WARRIOR

Max asked Claire to accompany him to the funeral. On some level this seemed an odd thing to be doing. He was taking along a woman he loved to the funeral of another he also loved. And besides that, she didn't really know Laura. Claire though was good about going and was very aware of how awkward it could prove to be, consequently, she told Max he should introduce her as his friend. She wanted to be there for Max and to pay her respects to Laura's family.

The funeral of Laura Aoife O'Donnell packed out the Chapel at the Banksia Funeral Home. It was a combination of rituals from both the NSW police department and her Irish heritage. Officers were in full uniform. A large window high up on the chapel wall was wide open to allow Laura's soul to return home. A large clay pot of tobacco smoldered away near the casket to ward off evil spirits.

At the front of the chapel on a low gold trolley was Laura's open casket. About half of the gathering had walked forward, knelt and uttered some quiet words before taking their seat. Max had not yet done so.

The catholic priest, Senior Sergeant David Heath and Laura's father, Connor, were the only ones to speak.

Connor's broad accent was beautiful and undulated wonderfully as he delivered the eulogy. Understanding him fully though was a challenge for most.

Claire had a tight grip on Max's right arm, and he had his left arm across himself hanging onto her.

With the completion of the service came the haunting song, "She Moved Through the Fair" as sung by Van Morrison.

The people were saying

No two e're were wed

But one has a sorrow

That never was said

And she smiled as she passed me

With her goods and her gear

And that was the last

That I saw of my dear…

Slowly the congregation made their way out of the chapel. Max remained seated at the end of the pew still clinging onto Claire as Laura's mother, Nessa, arrived next to him. She looked down on him with the kindest of smiles and extended her hand.

'Come,' she softly said.

As if in slow motion Max unwound himself from Claire, took Nessa's hand and rose to his feet. They walked forward to the casket.

'You must see her as she was meant to be seen,' said Nessa.

Max knelt at the casket still able to see inside. Nessa remained standing. Laura was dressed in long white linen pants and shirt with two buttons at the top and a collar. She had on white slippers. The tops of a dozen red roses were around her head like a halo. There were no marks on her neck or her wrists. She was whole again.

'Aoife, her middle name, means beautiful, radiant, joyful and the greatest of female warriors,' whispered Nessa. 'I'll leave you to say what you need to say.'

Tears dripped from his chin as he knelt looking at the beautiful Laura. Lying peacefully and looking splendid.

'I am so sorry... I regret so much. I never told you I loved you, but I did... so very much... You certainly know how to draw a crowd, so many friends and what a wonderful family. Wherever you are going, go there in peace and with my love.' He kissed his fingers and placed them against her cold lips. 'Goodbye my beautiful.'

*   *   *

The burial followed the service then everyone was invited to the large room adjacent to the chapel for a gathering and celebration of Laura's life. For those that had already peaked into the room this would include a large consumption of Irish whiskey – with bottles of Dingle, Red Spot and Knappogue Castle whiskies all lined up.

CHAPTER 51

THE NEW OLD DOCTOR

The bearded older man was well dressed underneath his open medical coat. A stethoscope hung around his neck and an ID badge was attached to his shirt pocket. He strolled along the hospital corridor. Ahead of him a policeman sat reading a magazine outside a single room.

As he arrived at the room, he placed a hand on the policeman's shoulder. 'Frank said you need to take a ten-minute coffee break.' The middle-aged policeman stood, gave a slight affirming nod and walked away.

As the doctor entered the room, he picked up a resuscitation bag from a trolley and placed it on the end of the bed. A dark-haired man with a drip in one arm and a plaster cast on the other was snoring lightly. The drip arm was handcuffed to the bedrail. Scrawled in red marker on a small whiteboard above the bed was the name Charles Halliday.

The doctor wheeled over a trifold privacy screen and opened it around the bed. Then he removed a syringe from his coat pocket and with his back to the patient pushed the needle into the lower part of the drip tubing. Halliday stirred.

'Hey doc,' said the sleepy patient. 'What's happening?'

'Some necessary medication.' The doctor expelled part of the drug then turned to face him.

Halliday looked at the contoured beard, the wrinkled face, the grey hair and the receding hairline. 'I know you,' he said. 'The airport! You're Judd...Max fucki...' He went to sit up and tried to lift his plastered arm but then fell back unable to move – unable to speak – unable to breathe. Dr Walter Rowbottom pushed in more of the drug. He put the manual resuscitator over Halliday's mouth and pumped it.

'I am giving you suxamethonium chloride. This is a good news bad news situation. The bad news is that it's a drug used in anesthesia that paralyses all your skeletal muscles. Huh, silly me,' quipped Walter as he flicked his head up and glanced at the ceiling. 'You must already know that, right? The good news is you can still see, hear and feel. And yes, a nice bonus too is that it only lasts around ten minutes, so you will be back to normal in no time. Well, unless I take this resuscitation bag away. Can a man hold his breath for ten minutes? Tricky. There's a challenge for you Halliday. And by the way you were right, Robert Mallory is very dead. Found his way into a tree mulcher. Can you believe that? He is very literally pushing up the daisies,' smiled the pretend doctor.

Walter took the bag away and expelled the last of the syringe contents. He placed two fingers on Halliday's neck and counted for a few seconds. 'One hundred and eighty! Oh, my goodness. You should see a doctor about that.' He stood a moment longer and watched as Halliday's complexion moved through stages of pink to red to crimson to purple.

Walter Rowbottom left. He would never be seen again.

CHAPTER 52

ALMOST 12 MONTHS LATER

On Monday the twenty-fifth of February 2019 Max knelt and placed twelve red roses against the headstone of Laura Aoife O'Donnell. In gold lettering on polished granite the simple epitaph read...

Deep peace of the quiet earth to you...

Laura Aoife O'Donnell

14ᵗʰ November 1989 – 25ᵗʰ February 2018

He moved from kneeling to sitting with his legs stretched out over the grass in front of the headstone.

'Not a day goes by when you are not in my thoughts,' he said softly. 'That will never change. It has been quite a year. And guess what? I have a regular, real paying job now...' he thought he heard a car door close. He looked around but could see no one and he was a good way from the carpark.

'You were right,' he continued. 'I am bored shitless. And Claire has sold Pelican Street and I sold my Melbourne unit. We bought a new house at Colebee in Western Sydney not far from the Uni. Double story with five bedrooms and some sort of backyard. The kids have visited. They really miss Fatso, Stretch and Stinkie.'

He took a deep breath, leaned back on his arms and looked to the clear blue sky.

'There you have it, *regular* old Max, a suburban clone. Who'd have thought? Claire seems happy enough. Keeps herself fit, still struggles with past events. It's a slow process. She might even get back to a teaching job soon. Our relationship is not quite what it used to be and that's understandable. It's different now. That's not necessarily a bad thing, just different that's all.'

There was another sound, like someone clearing their throat. Max sat up a little more. Then fifty metres away a man walked out from behind a line of trees that marked another row of gravestones. He moved slowly with his head down and his hands behind his back. He wore blue jeans, long sleeve check shirt, a baseball cap and sunnies.

Behind him, a further fifty metres away, stood two men in suits that seemed to be paying him some attention. The man moved closer. Max rose to his feet. His best exit may be weaving through the line of trees, heading to the gazebo and then down a grassy slope to the carpark.

The man was ten metres away when he raised his head showing a round boyish looking face. It was Ian Friend.

'What the hell,' muttered Max with some surprise. He was unsure what was happening. Jeremiah had said Ian would never *kill you himself*. Max hoped this was still true, but there were the other men further back.

Ian stopped two metres away and smiled. He moved his hands from behind his back. Max's adrenaline peaked ready for action, then he saw a bouquet of assorted coloured flowers and breathed a sigh of relief.

Ian stepped forward and placed the flowers next to the roses.

'Why are you here? Who are those men?' snapped Max.

'There is absolutely no threat here, Max,' said Ian as he stood back up and removed his sunglasses. 'It's been a year and I really wanted this day to come months ago, but it was impossible. I am truly sorry about that. I have been grieving with you, and for you, for all this time.' The counsellor looked at Max with his deep blue eyes and long eyelashes and spoke with that voice that carried such sincerity and compassion. Max knew it all so well and was not about to get lulled into a false sense of security.

'Fuck off!' he replied loudly.

'Do you think I tried to have you killed?' asked Ian.

'I know you did.'

'Do you think I was some wanna be drug baron?'

'I know you are.'

'Do you believe I was into race fixing?'

'I do not believe that,' Max shook his head. 'You are interrupting a deeply private moment here. You should leave.'

'I will,' said Ian. 'All your answers though are wrong, Max. I have been assisting the AFP with some undercover work. Currently I am in witness protection with my wife and son.'

Max just glared.

'You probably know Eli worked for me,' continued the counsellor. 'He was there at Oakdale when Frank turned up. If anyone tried to kill you, he would have put a bullet in their head.'

'You set me up with the Monaro. You sent Frank over to bust my balls!'

'Ezekiel asked you to get rid of it. When you didn't, he did the job for you. Then you planted it on me. Clever thinking. Could've got me killed.'

'Shame about that,' scoffed Max. 'You're trying to tell me that Ezekiel was an undercover operative too? Bullshit!'

'No. He was a patient of mine. Mentally unbalanced, but unique and so very clever and perceptive. He knew nothing of the AFP. But he was to look after you. My priority was for you to be safe. At the same time, I needed you off my case. The Feds were breathing down my neck. I needed to discredit myself in your eyes so you would be out of the picture. For a while the AFP wanted to take a closer look at you. I steered them back to Frank Mortimer.'

'Your personality just oozes generosity!' said Max. 'Fuck me!'

'I was involved in fixing races. All that stuff I told you was one hundred percent true.'

'I didn't believe any of it. Still don't.'

'I didn't want you to,' replied Ian.

'You wanted to make me believe you were lying. Are you fucking with me again?'

'I am here to tell you the truth.'

'There is no truth, just a different set of lies,' said Max.

'I was busted, Max. But they offered me immunity in exchange for information on Frank Mortimer. Frank had a hand in the racing thing as well. But the Feds wanted him for drugs and suspected murder. I never knew him personally. Never met him. The AFP sent Eli to see me supposedly for counselling. He knew Marco, one of

Frank's guys, who helped him get the security gig with Frank.'

'Why did the Feds need you?'

'I was more of a coordinator with Eli, the Feds and at times Ezekiel. I organised some cash drops, set up a few meetings and put together a few plans to rip off Frank's product.'

'You were manipulating your patients. Me included. Where are your standards? That is completely unethical.'

'Unfortunately, ethics and standards went out the window a long time ago.'

'You had Susan Mortimer killed,' said Max bluntly.

'No. I was aware she was going to die. And Ezekiel let me know when it happened.'

'Was this supposed to be a favour to me? Because that is pure crap. I am quite capable of doing my own dirty work.'

'Ezekiel believed that's what it was about, but really, Susan was about to bust open the whole case. She had identified an AFP agent.'

'Well fuck! That would be the islander? About thirty years old?'

'Yeah. That would be Aloisi.'

'The AFP organised a hit on someone? Really?'

'Frank would have found out. The case would have fallen apart. People might have died...' as soon as the words left his mouth, he realised what he had said. He dropped to his knees. 'Please forgive me. That was so wrong. Thoughtless. I meant no disrespect. Oh dear.'

'Ezekiel said you killed Laura by proxy.' Ian still referred to the hairless Bible buff as Ezekiel, there seemed no good reason to tell him otherwise.

Ian looked up at Max who remained standing looking down at him. The counsellor's complexion had changed. His face was flushed. His blue eyes were wet. 'I had nothing to do with her death…'

'Her murder,' interrupted Max.

'Yes, sorry. I had nothing at all to do with that.'

'Just like you had nothing to do with Susan Mortimer?'

'No. Not like that. I had no knowledge whatsoever. I swear that on the life of my wife and son. On my own life.'

The full details, including the horrific nature of Laura's death, had never been made public. It was known by her family, investigating police officers and a few select others. And no living person, other than Max, Jeremiah and Claire knew where she was murdered. It seemed most likely that Ian Friend would have no knowledge of this either. This is something he needs to know, thought Max. And this is something I very much want to tell him.

'When you sent Frank out to hassle me,' said Max, with a finger pointing and stabbing at the kneeling counsellor. 'Halliday was forced to change his agenda. The guy was following me just like I had planned. Then he gets the heads up that Frank and his mob were about to pay me a visit. So, he aborts the follow, and goes back for Laura.'

Ian's mouth hung open. 'What?' He swallowed heavily.

'He would have been on my bench, Ian!' continued Max at full throttle. 'Instead, Frank wrecks my security setup, and after he and his goons leave, Halliday comes back with Laura, having disabled her with a stun gun. He decapitates her in my bunker. Then chops both her hands off. He puts her severed head and hands on display, on the dining room table of my apartment. What do you think about them apples counsellor?'

Ian fell forward onto the grass in front of the gravestone. He sobbed. The two suited men made a move. Max remained standing over Ian as the two men arrived. One had a hand inside his coat.

'What's going on? Ian are you all right?' yelled one of the men.

Ian rolled over, nodded and held up an open hand. The two suits looked around checking for onlookers. There were none. 'We need to go,' said the gun happy suit.

Ian dragged himself to his feet. 'Give us one more minute, please.'

'One minute, then we leave,' said the officer. The two suits backed away.

'If I had only known…'

'I thought we were the best of friends,' snapped Max. 'You have let me down in ways that go beyond description. I don't know whether I can ever forgive you. We could've sat down, just you and me, somewhere away from prying eyes. We could've worked this out.'

The counsellor panted and rubbed his eyes.

'I have no words,' he blubbered.

'That's a first.'

'I have failed you. You, others, myself.'

'All this,' continued Max. 'All this mayhem, this killing. For what? What is there to show for it?'

'There is evidence. Hard evidence against Mortimer.' Ian wiped his eyes.

'But?'

'They want to wait. A big shipment is coming. Any day.'

'There's always a shipment coming. Your minute is up. You should go now. Leave me. I need to spend some quiet time with Laura.'

Ian Friend left with his two escorts. Max squatted then grabbed the bunch of flowers and threw them to one side.

Maxwell Judd continued to talk with Laura. He was choked up and a bit teary, but he was in control. Even his anger with Ian had declined as soon as the counsellor left. He reflected on his conversation and smiled to himself as he decided it was one of his better counselling sessions. He had offloaded a good deal of hurt and it felt relieving. Also, he had heard some version of the truth. The story bothered him little and he felt no desire to pursue it any further.

He lay down stretched out on the grass with the top of his head against Laura's gravestone.

'Regular Max, Laura,' he said. 'Regular boring Max. And I think I'm gonna be okay with it.'

****

ABOUT THE AUTHOR

Bob Goodwin was born in Nottingham, England and moved to Australia when he was 7 years old. He has spent over 35 years working in various areas of mental health – including Psychiatric Institutions, Mental Health Inpatient Units, Community Mental Health Services, Mental Health Rehab & Residential facilities and Telephone services for Mental Health Triage.

Bob started writing in 1987 and, aside from his novels, he has written several One Act Plays, short plays, feature length screenplays and short stories.

Other fiction novels by Bob Goodwin:

Strike Me Dead (2014)

The 13th Black Candle (2015)

Max Justice (2016) Book 1 in the Max Judd series

Max Justice: Turmoil (2017) Book 2 in the Max Judd series

All available as a paperback or in digital formats.

Catch up with Bob at:

> http://storiesandplays.com/ ,or https://www.amazon.com/-/e/B00JC3SHIS

You can also follow or comment on Twitter

> https://twitter.com/GoodOneBob

On Instagram at:

> https://www.instagram.com/goodonebob/?hl=en

And via Facebook "Writers & Readers" or Bob's author page:

> https://www.facebook.com/groups/140516869352008/

> https://www.facebook.com/Bob-Goodwin-Author-989354194414457/

ACKNOWLEDGEMENTS

Thanks Jenny, for your read, feedback and corrections

To Judy for her editing and positive comments.

To Ian for his pre-print read.

The city of Sydney and surrounds. I will be a regular visitor.

To Google Earth who took me to so many locations without complaining.

To all my friends and readers for their continued support and encouragement.

To Spiffing Covers for their superb work on the book cover.

www.ingramcontent.com/pod-product-compliance
Lightning Source LLC
Chambersburg PA
CBHW071454170626
46811CB00007B/2576